NATIONAL SCIENCE OLYMPIAD

Exploring the World of Science

Class 2

Shikha Gupta
Shikha Nautiyal

V&S PUBLISHERS

Published by:

V&S PUBLISHERS

F-2/16, Ansari road, Daryaganj, New Delhi-110002
☎ 23240026, 23240027 • *Fax:* 011-23240028
Email: info@vspublishers.com • *Website:* www.vspublishers.com

Regional Office : Hyderabad

5-1-707/1, Brij Bhawan (Beside Central Bank of India Lane)
Bank Street, Koti, Hyderabad - 500 095
☎ 040-24737290
E-mail: vspublishershyd@gmail.com

Branch Office : Mumbai

Jaywant Industrial Estate, 1st Floor–108, Tardeo Road
Opposite Sobo Central Mall, Mumbai – 400 034
☎ 022-23510736
E-mail: vspublishersmum@gmail.com

Follow us on:

All books available at **www.vspublishers.com**

© **Copyright:** *V&S* PUBLISHERS
ISBN 978-93-579404-1-2

Printed at : Param Offseters Okhla New Delhi-110020

Publisher's Note

V&S Publishers, after the grand success of a number of Academic and General books, is pleased to bring out a series of *Science Olympiad books* under *The Gen X series – generating Xcellence in generation X –* which has been designed to focus the problems faced by students. In all books the concepts have been explained clearly through various examples, illustrations and diagrams wherever required. Each book has been developed to meet specific needs of students who aspire to get distinctions in the field of science and want to become Olympiad champs at national level.

To go through the exams successfully, the students need to do thorough study of topics covered in the *Olympiad syllabus and the topics covered in the school syllabus as well.* The Olympiads not only tests subjective knowledge but Reasoning skills of the students also. So students are required to comprehend the depth of concepts. The Olympiads check efficiency of candidates in problem solving. These exams are conducted in different stages at regional, national, and international levels. At each stage of the exam, the candidate should be fully prepared to go through the exam. Therefore, this test requires careful attention towards comprehension of concepts, thorough practice, and application of rules.

While other books in market focus selectively on questions or theory; V&S Science Olympiad books are rather comprehensive. Each book has been divided into five sections namely *Science, Logical Reasoning, Achievers section, Subjective section, and Model Papers.* The theory has been explained through solved examples. To enhance problem solving skills of candidates, *Multiple Choice Questions (MCQs)* with detailed solutions are given at the end of each chapter. Two *Mock Test Papers* have been included to understand the pattern of exam. A CD containing Study Chart for systematic preparation, Tips & Tricks to crack Science Olympiad, Pattern of exam, and links of Previous Years Papers is accompanied with this book. The books are also useful for various other competitive exams such as NTSE, NSTSE, and SLSTSE as well.

We wish you all success in the Olympiad and a very bright future in the field of science. All the best

Contents

Section 1: Science

Section 2: Logical Reasoning

Section 3: Achievers Section

Section 4: Subjective Section

Section 5: Model Papers

Section 1: Science

Plants

> ## Learning milestones:
> ❑ Types of plants
> ❑ Plants and their habitats
> ❑ Parts of a plant
> ❑ Uses of plants

We see different types of plants around us. Some plants are big and some are small. Some have flowers and some are completely green.

Types of Plants

Depending on their size, plants are of three types: Trees, shrubs, and herbs.

Trees

Big and tall plants are called trees. They have thick, strong, and woody stem. This stem is called the **trunk**. Trees have a long life and live for many years. For example: mango, banyan, peepal, and bamboo.

Some trees like neem and peepal shed their leaves every year. They are called **deciduous trees**. Some trees like mango ad banyan remain green throughout the year. They are called **evergreen trees**.

Shrubs

Shrubs are smaller than trees. They have thick stems but they are not as thick as the stems of trees. Shrubs are also called **bushes**. They are generally low in height and only live for a few years. China Rose (hibiscus), rose, cotton, and tulsi (basil) are examples of shrubs.

Herbs

Herbs are very small plants as compared to trees and shrubs. They have green and soft stems. Coriander, mustard, spinach, and mint are some example of herbs.

Many herbs live for a year or only a couple of months.

Climbers

A climber is a plant which has a weak stem. The stem coils around a support to grow straight. Money plant, bitter gourd, grape, and pea plant are a few examples of climbers. Climbers generally live for a few months, but some may live for years.

Creepers

A creeper is a plant which grows along the ground. It has weak and thin stems. Plants like cucumber, pumpkin, and watermelon are creepers.

Thorny Plants

Some plants which have thorns are called thorny plants. Cactus, acacia, and rose plants are all thorny plants.

Plant Habitat

Plants can be found both on land and in water. Different plants live in different habitats.

> **Do you know?**
> A habitat is a special place where a plant or animal lives.

Some plants grow on land, some in water, some in very hot regions, whereas some grow in very cold regions.

> **Do you know?**
> Short grasses usually grow in cold, dry climates on high mountains. Their leaves are small and tough-bladed that keep the water in.

Plants can be classified in various categories:

a. Plants that grow on land

    1. Plants that grow on mountains and hills: These plants are tall, sturdy, and coniferous. Examples: Cedar, Pine Spruce, conifers, fir

2. Plants that grow in warm places or plains: These plants have many leaves and are shady. Most of the trees that grow in warm places or plains shed leaves in autumn.

   Example: Banyan, Mango, Papaya, Neem

3. Plants that grow in deserts or dry regions: These plants are adapted to living in hot and dry conditions. They have thick stems and spines all over their body. They lose very little water.

   Example: Saguaro, Prickly pear, Agave, Hedgehog

b. Plants that grow in water

Plants that grow in water are called **aquatic plants**. They possess specific characteristics to survive in water.

Test Your Skills

1. Which plant will dry sooner in summer?

2. Which of these plants needs the most water?

3. Which of these is a seasonal plant?

Parts of a Plant

A plant has many parts. The following are the various parts of a plant:

Root: They grow under the ground. Roots collect water and minerals from the soil for the plant.

Stem: The stem grows above the ground. It is the main body of a plant. It transports food and water to all parts of the plant.

Leaves: They make food for the plant.

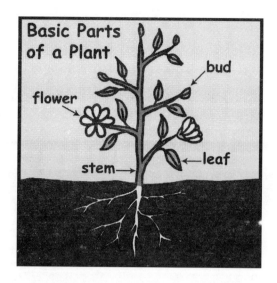

Basic Parts of a Plant

flower, bud, stem, leaf

Do you know?

Green plants are the only living things that can produce food. They are able to do so because of the presence of a substance called chlorophyll in their leaves. Chlorophyll is green in colour. It is also responsible for imparting green colour to the leaves.

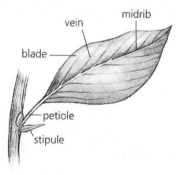

blade, vein, midrib, petiole, stipule

Flowers: They produce fruit.

Fruits: They have seeds in them. A baby plant grows from a seed. Plants need air, soil, water, and sunlight for their growth.

Test Your Skills

Define the functions of the following in one line:

1. Stem
2. Root
3. Leaves
4. Seed

Plants Give us Food

Most of our food comes from plants. Plants make their own food. Leaves are the food factories of the plants and the food is stored in different parts of the plant.

Roots: We eat the root of plants like radish, carrot, turnip, and beetroot.

Stems: We eat stems of plants like ginger, potato, and sugarcane.

Leaves: Leaves of some plants are eaten as vegetables. For example: cabbage, spinach, fenugreek, and mint.

Flowers: We eat flowers of plants like broccoli and cauliflower.

Seeds: We eat seeds of many plants like gram, beans, corn, and peas. Food grains like cereals and pulses are also seeds of the plants.

Fruits: Fruits of some plants are eaten as vegetables.
We all enjoy eating juicy fruits like mangoes, grapes, apples, and oranges.

Plants Give us Spices

Spices add taste and flavour to the food. Plants give us spices like chilies, peppercorns, cardamom, turmeric, and coriander seeds.

Plants Give us Oilseeds

We get oil from plants. Seeds containing oil are called oilseeds. This oil is used for various things, including cooking food and for applying on the body.

Plants Give us Tea, Coffee, Sugar, and Cocoa

We get tea from the leaves of a tea plant.

Coffee beans, from the coffee plant, are crushed to make coffee powder.

Sugarcane juice, from the sugarcane plant, is used to make sugar.

Seeds of cocoa tree are crushed to make cocoa powder.

Plants Also Give us:

♦ Plants give us oxygen. Trees and plants make the air fresh by giving out oxygen and taking in carbon dioxide.

♦ Plants add beauty to our surroundings.

♦ Plants provide shelter.

♦ Green trees and plants are home to many animals like monkeys, squirrels, birds, and insects. Plants provide fodder for animals.

♦ Plants give fibers. We get fibers like cotton, jute, flax, and coir from the plants. Cotton fibers are used to make cotton clothes. Jute fiber is used to make bags and ropes.

♦ Plants give us manure. Dry leaves are mixed with soil to make manure. Plants that grow in this soil are very healthy and strong.

♦ Plants give wood and many other things like medicine, paper, gum, and rubber.

Multiple Choice Questions

1. **Very small plants that have soft stems are called:**
   - A. Herbs
   - B. Trees
   - C. Shrubs
   - D. Climbers

2. **Plant that creep on the ground:**
   - A. Jackfruit
   - B. Watermelon
   - C. Rose
   - D. Pineapple

3. **A tree stem is protected by an outer covering called:**
   - A. Branch
   - B. Cork
   - C. Bark
   - D. Trunk

4. **Brinjal plant is a:**
   - A. Herb
   - B. Shrub
   - C. Tree
   - D. None of these

5. **Which of these plant live for only one season?**
   - A. Mango
   - B. Guava
   - C. Rubber plant
   - D. Rice

Based on the image below answer question number 6–8

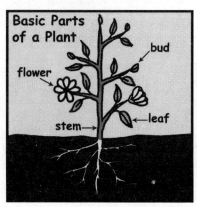

6. **Which part of the plant helps in transpiration?**
   - A. Stem
   - B. Leaves
   - C. Roots
   - D. Branches

7. **Which part of a plant helps in photosynthesis or the production of sugar and release of oxygen?**
   - A. Roots
   - B. Flowers
   - C. Stem
   - D. Leaves

8. **Which part of a plant helps in transporting the nutrients from the soil?**
   A. Roots
   B. Flowers
   C. Stem
   D. Leaves

9. **The correct order of a plant's life cycle is:**
   A. Seed, sprout, seedling, plant, and flower
   B. Sprout, seed, seedling, plant, and flower
   C. Flower, seed, seedling, sprout, and plant
   D. Flower, seed, seedling, and sprout

10. **Cactus plants are part of which of the following plant categories?**
    A. Aquatic plants
    B. Coniferous plants
    C. Deciduous plants
    D. Desert plants

11. **Which is the odd plant among the following?**

A.

B.

C.

D.

12. **Which of these is not a desert plant feature?**
    A. Spines
    B. No leaves
    C. Thick spongy stem
    D. Lots of flowers

13. **Plants that grow on land are called:**
    A. Aquatic plants
    B. Coniferous plants
    C. Terrestrial plants
    D. Xerophytes

14. **Floating and fixed plants are a variety of:**
    A. Aquatic plants
    B. Coniferous plants
    C. Terrestrial plants
    D. Xerophytes

15. **Trees on plains do not have which of these characteristics?**
    A. Autumn shedding of leaves
    B. Lots of stomata
    C. Lots of leaves
    D. Adapted to high heat and dry conditions

16. **Which of these is not a thorny plant?**
    A. Jackfruit
    B. Lemon
    C. Bougainvillea
    D. Prickly pear

17. **Thorns of which of these plants are actually reduced leaves?**
    A. Rose
    B. Lemon
    C. Bougainvillea
    D. Prickly pear

18. **Broad, waxy leaves are found in:**
    A. Cactus
    B. Banyan
    C. Hibiscus
    D. Water lily

19. **Which of the following plants correctly matches the given description?**
    I am a small plant.
    I have a number of roots growing from the base of my stem.
    I am seasonal.
    A. Wheat
    C. Carrot
    B. Mango tree
    D. Rose

20. **Raghu is classifying some vegetables according to the part of the plant that we eat. He has done a mistake. Which vegetable is wrongly classified?**

Vegetable	Part of the plant
Carrot	Stem
Cabbage	Leaves
Potato	Flower
Cauliflower	Flower
Beetroot	Root
Onion	Leaves
Brinjal	Fruit

A. Brinjal   B. Onion and potato

C. Cabbage   D. Carrot

21. **Kartik was confused when his father asked him which plant fibre is stuffed in his pillow. Help him name it.**

A. Jute   B. Coconut

C. Wool   D. Cotton

22. **What are the similarities between the two plants given below:**

A. They both have thick, woody stems

B. They are creepers

C. They are herbs

D. They have weak, soft stems

23. **Ravi planted two plants in two pots. Plant A had no roots while plant B had no leaves. Which plant will die?**

A. Plant A and B both will die because they do not have roots and leaves, respectively

B. Plant A will die because roots are important to take up nutrition from soil and helps in plant growth

C. Plant B will die because leaves are important for making food

D. Nor plant A neither plant B will die

24. Which of the following is important for a plant?

A.

B.

C.

D.

Answer Key

1. A   2. B   3. C   4. A   5. D   6. B   7. D   8. C   9. A

10. D   11. A   12. D   13. C   14. A   15. D   16. A   17. D   18. D

19. A   20. B   21. D   22. D   23. B   24. B

Animals

> ## Learning milestones:
> ☐ Wild Animals
> ☐ Domestic Animals

Wild Animals

Animals are found everywhere.

Animals that live in forests are called **wild animals**. There are many kinds of wild animals. Some of these are very big and some are small.

Homes for wild animals

Wild animals live in natural shelters or they build their own houses.

Tigers and lions live in dens. Elephants live under trees and monkeys live on the trees.

Some animals live in holes under the ground. These underground holes are called **burrows**. Rats, snakes, moles, mongoose, and rabbits live in burrows.

Birds live in trees. They make nests for laying eggs. They also raise their babies in the nests till the baby birds grow up and are able to fly. Cuckoos do not make nests. They lay their eggs in a crow's nest.

What do Wild Animals Eat?

Animals eat different kinds of food.

Some animals eat only plants. This means they eat leaves, flowers, fruits, or even wood. For example, a parrot eats fruits and nuts.

These animals are called **herbivores.** Cows, goats, elephants, horses, giraffes, etc., are all herbivores. Herbivores have sharp, broad teeth for chewing grass.

There are some animals that mainly eat seeds. They are called **granivores.**

Then there are animals that mainly eat foliage. Such animals are called **folivores.**

Some animals consume other animals. These animals are called **carnivores**. A carnivore is a predator because it has to find and catch its prey. They have strong teeth on the sides of their mouth. These teeth are called **canines**. They are sharp enough to bite into the flesh.

Then there are those animals that eat both plants and animals. These animals are called **omnivores.** Animals like dogs, bears, cats, etc., are all omnivores. Chickens are also omnivorous. They eat seeds but they also eat worms. Chimpanzees are also omnivorous.

One type of carnivore is **scavengers**. Animals like hyenas and jackals are scavengers. They do not kill animals themselves, but instead feed on flesh of dead animals.

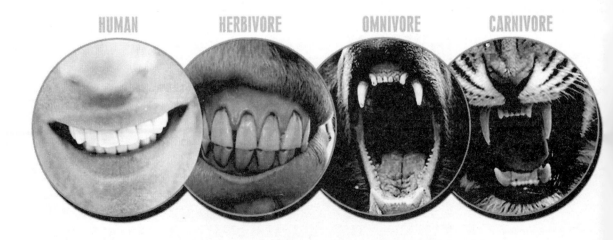

HUMAN   HERBIVORE   OMNIVORE   CARNIVORE

Do you know?

Leafcutter ants are different from other species of ants in the way they make their food. They get their name because of their ability to cut leaves from trees with their scissor-like mandibles. Once leaves are cut, each ant carries a leaf back to the colony where the leaves are added to a pile, similar to a compost heap.

Saving Wild Animals

Cutting down of trees in the forests destroys the homes of wild animals. Animals such as leopards and rhinoceros are also hunted and killed for their skin and horns.

Zoos and sanctuaries are made to save and protect wild animals. A wildlife sanctuary is a space which is set aside exclusively for wild animals, which are protected when they roam or live in that area.

Government and private organizations help in protecting these wild animals.

One such organization is World Wildlife Federation (WWF), which is involved in protecting and restoring species and their habitats. The World Wildlife Fund was conceived in April, 1961.

Domestic Animals

Animals like dogs, cows, cats, crows, sparrows, and goats, live in our houses or near our houses. They are called domestic animals.

Domestic animals are divided into two groups – companion animals and farm animals.

1. **Companion animals** are those animals which give human beings company. They become our friends and part of our family.

2. **Farm animals** are those animals which are tamed by us. They help us in many ways.

Domestic Animals give us Milk, Eggs, and Flesh

Milk: Cow, goat, buffalo, camel.

Milch Animals

Cow

Buffalo

Goat

Eggs: Hen, duck, turkey, goose.

Meat: Goat, pig, hen, duck, fish.

Animals that provide fibre and leather

Animals give us fibres like wool and silk. Sheep give us wool and silkworms give us silk. Skin of some animals is used to produce leather after they are dead. Animals that give us leather are camel, elephant, crocodile, and buffalo.

Other useful animals

1. Animals like oxen and camels are used to **plough** agricultural farmlands in villages.

2. Animals help us to **carry load.** In ancient times when there were no trucks and modern means of transport, animals like elephants, donkeys, horses, and camels

were used as load carrying animals. We still see many such animals carrying loads for human beings.

3. Animals are used for **riding and transportation in carts**, like horse carts, bullock carts, and camel carts.

4. **Animal dung** is used as **manure and fuel**. For example, cow dung is used as fuel.

5. Dogs help **guard houses** and **other farm animals**.

6. We keep some animals at home as our **pets**. We love them and care for them. They too love us. Dogs and cats are common pets. Some people keep birds such as parrots, mynahs as pets.

Test Your Skills

Follow the instruction to solve the puzzle. The puzzle has animal shelter names hidden in it:

1. Circle every fourth letter to get my name:

APINORSEGKMSBNJT

2. Early man lived in me. Who am I?

3. Read my name backwards: **ELOH**

4. If you destroy me, you will lose jungles. Who am I?

Multiple Choice Questions

1. **Which of these kill other animals for food?**

A.
B.

C.
D.

2. **Which of these help to keep the jungles clean by eating dead animals?**

A.
B.

C.
D.

3. **Which of these wild animals are herbivores?**
   A. Elephants
   B. Black bear
   C. Monkeys
   D. All of them

4. **Who am I?**
   I am a big animal with big ears and a trunk. I love to eat sugarcane.
   A. Herbivore
   B. Plant eater
   C. Carnivore
   D. A and B both

5. **To help keep unwanted animals away from your home:**
    A. Leave bowls of pet food on the doorway
    B. Keep garbage in tightly covered garbage cans
    C. Keep water in buckets nearby
    D. None of the above

6. **If you are bitten or scratched by an animal, you should:**
    A. Wash the wound with lots of soap and water
    B. Tell an adult
    C. Chase the animal
    D. A and B both

7. **Animals that most often get rabies are:**
    A. Cats
    B. Dogs
    C. Monkeys, cats, and dogs
    D. Lizards

8. **Which of these animals gives us leather?**
    A. Snake   b. Ant
    C. Fish   d. Sheep

9. **Which of these animals gives us honey?**
    A. Housefly   B. Bee
    C. Mosquito   D. Butterfly

10. **Which of the following statements is correct?**
    A. Some animals have sharp front teeth both in upper and lower jaws to break open fruits and nuts
    B. Grass eating animals have strong broad back teeth to grind their food
    C. Flesh-eating animals have pointed teeth to tear flesh
    D. All of the above statements are correct

11. **Which of these is a wrong match?**
    A. Crows-caw
    B. Cows-bark
    C. Cats-meow
    D. Sparrows-chirp

12. **In the given image, who is the herbivore?**

A. Frog
b. Snake
C. Caterpillar
d. None of them

13. **In the given image, who is the most important?**

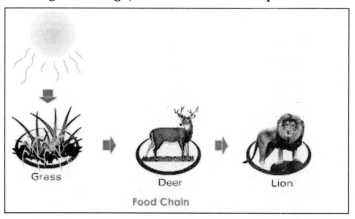

A. Deer
B. Lion
C. Plant
D. All of them

14. **Which of the following lay eggs?**

A. 
B.

C. 
D.

15. We get this from animals:

A.

B.

C.

D. A and C

16. Which of the following have webbed feet?

A   Elephants   B   Snake
C   Ducks   D   Sparrow

17. An animal lives in water, eats other animals, and gives birth to babies in water. Who is this animal?

A   Shark   B. Whale
C. Dolphin   D. Crocodile

18. Which animal's offspring is called a "calf".

A   Dog   B. Cow, dolphin, elephant
C. Bear   D. Duck

19. **Deer are eaten by:**

    A. Herbivores
    B. Carnivores
    C. Omnivores
    D. Both B and C

20. **What is common among the following animals?**

    A. They lay eggs and have wings
    B. They have wings
    C. They lay eggs
    D. They are carnivores

21. **What is common among the following animals?**

    A. They give us useful products like milk
    B. They are farm animals
    C. They can be tamed
    D. All of the above

22. **Which is the correct match?**

I	II
A. Buffalo	i. Egg giving animal
B. Goat	ii. Meat giving animal
C. Lion	iii. Milk giving domestic animal
D. Hen	iv. Wild carnivore

    A. A (iii), B (ii), C (iv), D (i)
    B. A (ii), B (iii), C (i), D (iv)

C. A (i), B (ii), C (iv), D (iii)

D. A (iii), B (i), C (iv), D (ii)

23. **Read the poem below and find out what is wrong.**

Monkeys can jump and climb trees

Giraffes are short and they eat leaves

Parrots are colourful and they can fly

Elephants can't but would love to try.

Turtles are green and they can swim

Cheetahs can run and they always win

Zebras look like horses but they are black and white

Hippos are big and snore at night.

A. Turtles cannot swim   B. Zebras resemble cows

C. Giraffes are not short   D. Parrots are not colourful

24. **White tigers are:**

A. Extinct   B. Endangered

C. Protected   D. Endangered and threatened

25. **Identify the bird given in the picture below. Name the country whose national animal this bird is.**

A. Kiwi, Australia   B. Kiwi, New Zeland

C. Penguin, Australia   D. Kiwi, America

Answer Key

1. A   2. C   3. D   4. D   5. B   6. D   7. C   8. A   9. B 10
D11. B   12. C   13. D   14. A   15. D   16. C   17. C   18. B   19. D 20
A21. D   22. A   23. C   24. D   25. B

Human Body

> ## Learning milestones:
> ☐ *Our body*
>   ☐ *External body organs*
>   ☐ *Sensory organs*
>   ☐ *Internal body organs*
> ☐ *Bones and muscles of our body*
> ☐ *Keeping bones and muscles healthy*

Our Body

Our body is important because it is unique–the only one of its kind. Our body grows, moves, and feels. It has five senses–hearing, seeing, touching, tasting, and smelling. There is a special part in our body that lets us think and have feelings. This is the brain. We look after our body by eating healthy food, exercising, resting, and keeping it clean.

External Body Organs

The following are the external body organs:

Head: The head consists of the eyes, nose, mouth, forehead, ears, cheek, and chin.

Neck: The neck consists of the shoulders.

Arm: The arm consists of the elbow, wrist, fingers, and thumb.

Spine: The spine consists of the chest and the thorax.

Leg: The leg consists of the knee, ankle, foot, and toes.

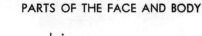

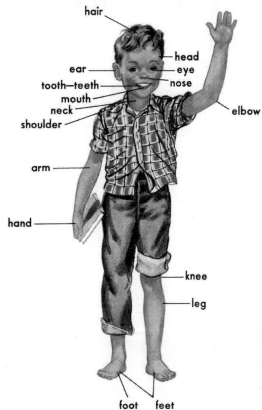

PARTS OF THE FACE AND BODY

Sensory Organs

Our senses are the physical means by which we see, hear, smell, and touch (feel).

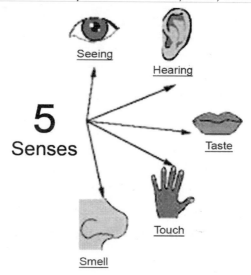

Eye: Sight

The sense of sight helps us recognize each other and learn about colour, motion, and distance. Eyes are our "sense of sight" organs.

> **Do you know?**
>
> Are tears important? Why?
>
> Yes, they keep your eyes wet, but they also help them stay clean.

Ear: Hearing

The sense of hearing helps us hear and respond through communication. Ears are our hearing organs. The ear also helps us maintain our balance.

Skin: Touch

This sensory organ is used to touch and feel things. We can feel when something is hot or cold, whether something is smooth, rough, hard, or soft. We can also tell when someone is touching us or when something is placed on our skin.

Nose: Smell

The nose helps us in smelling things and it's a big part of why we are able to taste different food.

Tongue: Taste

Taste helps us select and enjoy food. There are four familiar tastes: Sweet, Sour, Salty, and Bitter. The tongue also helps us with our speech.

Do you know?

The tongue is the main part of the body you use for tasting food. It carries messages to the brain about the taste of what you are eating. Inside your mouth are small bundles called taste buds. These are groups of sensory cells with many nerve endings, just like the nerve fibers in your nose. They detect the taste of the food you are eating or the fluid you are drinking.

Taste buds are stimulated by chemicals that dissolve in the saliva. The four kinds of tastes are salty, sour, sweet, and bitter.

Test Your Skills

Read the names of food items given below and write down how they taste?

♦ Cookie

♦ Lemon

♦ Cracker

♦ Banana

Internal Organs

Internal organs are the organs which we cannot see with eyes as they are inside our body. Following are the different internal organs of our body:

Brain

Brain controls our body and everything it does. Our brain makes us who we are.

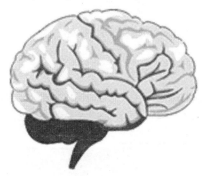

The Brain

Do you know?

The brain only weighs 1.4–1.8 kgs. This is about the weight of an average text book but it is the most complex object in the world.

Heart

The heart's job is to keep us alive by pumping blood through our body.

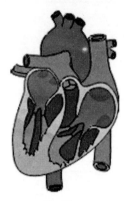

The Heart

Stomach

The stomach is where our food goes. Stomach helps in digestion of food.

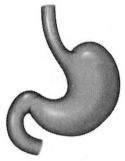

The Stomach

The Liver

The liver has many jobs but its main job is to filter out all the poisonous substances from our blood.

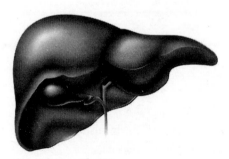

The Liver

Lungs

The lungs are the organs that help us breathe. We take in oxygen though our nose which goes into the lungs and we give out carbon dioxide.

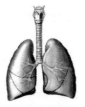

The Lungs

Kidneys

The kidneys help us get rid of wastes present in our bodies. It is called an excretory organ.

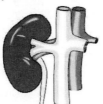

The Kidney

Test Your Skills

In the following puzzle, different parts of the body are hidden. Find them and write them in the blanks:

S	T	O	M	A	C	H
K	O	T	O	E	P	E
I	N	L	U	N	G	A
N	G	I	T	E	A	R
O	U	M	H	I	K	T
S	E	B	H	E	A	D
E	Y	E	H	A	N	D

1. _____
2. _____
3. _____
4. _____
5. _____
6. _____
7. _____

Bones and Muscles of Our Body

Our body is made up of blood, bones, and muscles. Bones and muscles work together to make our body work like a machine.

Our body is exactly like a clay idol. The strong frame of our body is made up of bones.

Bones

Bones are usually very hard. There are 206 bones in our body. All the bones in our body form a framework called the skeleton. Bones give protection to the internal organs of our body such as heart, brain, lungs, kidneys, and stomach. They also give shape to our body.

Do you know?

At birth, humans have 300 bones.

As a baby grows, however, many of the smaller bones fuse together, hence adults have just 206 bones.

Joints

Keep a book on the floor. Now try to pick it up without bending your knees or back. Same like a book, we have to bend our body to do many activities. Joint is a place where two or more bones meet. Joints are the only parts of the body where we can bend. There are 230 joints in our body.

Test Your Skills

Which part of his body is affected and what is the significance of part?

Muscles

There are about 650 muscles in our body. Muscles are very soft and are attached to the bones. Bones and muscles work together to move all the parts of our body. When we run, walk, or sit, our muscles pull our bones and help us perform such actions.

National Science Olympiad – Class 2

Keeping Bones and Muscles Healthy

Our bones and muscles help us move our body so we should take good care of them.

Exercise: To keep our bones and muscles healthy, we must exercise regularly. Running, sleeping, swimming, and cycling are some exercises which make our muscles strong.

Jogging

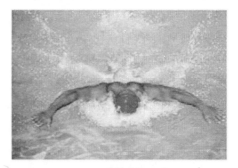
Swimming

Food: A diet rich in proteins helps in building muscles. Milk and milk products like cheese, curd, ghee, etc. keep our bones strong. Sunlight is also good for our bones.

Posture: Posture is the position of our body when we sit, stand, or move. While sitting, standing, or walking, we must keep our back straight. A wrong posture can spoil the shape of our bones and muscles.

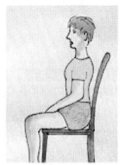

Boy Sitting On A Chair With Back Straight

Girl Standing Straight

Woman Walking With Back Straight

Multiple Choice Questions

1. **The limbs which helps us to hold something are called:**
   A. Arms
   B. Toes
   C. Hands
   D. Legs

2. **Which is the largest sensory organ?**
   A. Ears
   B. Skin
   C. Tongue
   D. Eyes

3. **Which organ helps maintain our body temperature?**
   A. Ears
   B. Skin
   C. Tongue
   D. Eyes

4. **The body parts which can be seen are called:**
   A. External organs
   B. Internal organs
   C. Spare organs
   D. Mobile organs

5. **The body parts which are functioning internally and cannot be seen outside are called:**
   A. Internal organs
   B. External organs
   C. Extreme organs
   D. Intertwined organs

6. **The organ which gives shape to our body is called the:**
   A. Skeleton
   B. Skin
   C. Heart
   D. Lungs

7. **Which is the organ that filters the blood and releases waste substance in the form of urine?**
   A. Kidneys
   B. Skin
   C. Heart
   D. Lungs

8. **Brain is protected by a hard bony cover called the:**
   A. Skeleton
   B. Skull
   C. Rib cage
   D. Skin

9. **Lungs are protected by the:**
   A. Skeleton
   B. Skull
   C. Rib cage
   D. Skin

10. **The master organ of our body is the:**
    A. Heart
    B. Lungs
    C. Stomach
    D. Brain

11. **Our eye is our organ for our sense of _____.**
    A. Smell
    b. Hearing
    C. Vision
    d. Touch

12. **You hear sounds through:**
    A. Vibration
    b. Music
    C. Noise
    d. Light

13. **Your _____ are groups of cells inside your mouth that detect the taste of the food you eat.**
    A. Tongue
    b. Teeth
    C. Taste buds
    d. Saliva

14. **Which sense do you use to detect which perfume has good odour?**
    A. Taste
    B. Smell
    C. Sight
    D. Touch

15. **Which body parts are used by the girl in the picture:**

    A. Only legs
    B. Only hands
    C. Facial expressions
    D. Whole body

16. **Hearing disability may happen due to:**
    A. Loud noise
    B. Loud music
    C. Sound of crackers
    D. All of these

17. **In which of the following activities do we use our body the least:**
    A. Sleeping
    B. Jumping
    C. Singing
    D. Eating

18. **Which of the following statements is correct?**
    A. Our bones are covered with muscles
    B. Muscles help us move
    C. There are more than 600 muscles in our body
    D. All of the above

19. **The place where two or more bones are joined are called:**
    A. Muscles   B. Tendon
    C. Joint   D. Elbows

20. **In the following, whose heart will beat the fastest?**
    A. Neha is sitting
    B. Rohan is running
    C. Preeti is standing
    D. Gauri is reading

21. **The role of the organ given below is:**

    A. Pump blood   B. Think and act
    C. Taste food   D. Excrete waste

22. **Good posture keeps our back pain free. Which of the following is not a good posture?**

A.    B.

C.    D.

23. **Which part of the body can we bend?**
    A. Knee   B. Elbow
    C. Both A and B   D. Rib cage

24. **Which of the following is not a sensory organ:**
    A. Stomach   B. Tongue
    C. Finger tips   D. Eyes

25. **Identify this joint:**

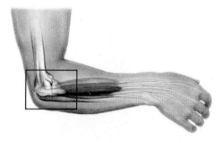

    A. Knee   B. Elbow
    C. Hip   D. Shoulder

Answer Key

1. C	2. B	3. B	4. A	5. A	6. A	7. A	8. B	9. C
10. D	11. C	12. A	13. C	14. B	15. D	16. D	17. A	18. D
19. C	20. B	21. A	22. A	23. C	24. A	25. B		

Food

Learning milestones:
- ☐ Different kinds of food
- ☐ Healthy eating habits
- ☐ Healthy teeth

Food

We all need food to live and grow. Human beings enjoy eating various types of food, which come from different sources. Almost all foods are of plant or animal origin. Like animals, human beings are also 'consumers', since they cannot produce their own food.

Different Kinds of Food

Different kinds of food help us in different ways.

Some Foods Give us Energy

Energy is required to work, play, study, and do all our daily activities. Imagine what will happen if we do not eat food for one whole day?

We will feel weak. This is the reason why we need energy-giving food.

Cereals, roots and tubers, dried fruits, oils, butter, and ghee are all good sources of energy.

Some Foods Help us Grow

Milk, meat, eggs, and fish are rich in high-quality proteins. Protein helps us to grow. Pulses and nuts are good sources of protein but the protein found in these food items is not of high quality. The protein found in eggs is considered to be the best protein.

Some Foods Keep us Healthy

Some foods like fruits and vegetable prevent us from falling sick.

They are essential for health and regulate activities like maintaining the heartbeat. These foods help us fight against diseases and make us healthy. They are also called protective foods.

Sources of protective and regulatory food are:

Healthy Eating Habits

There are certain things we need to keep in our mind when we eat food and drink water.

1. We must wash our hands with soap and water and rinse our mouth with water before and after every meal.

2. We must eat food slowly and chew it well.
3. We must eat our food at a fixed time daily. Dinner should be at about 7 pm in the evening.
4. We should never skip breakfast before going to school.
5. We must drink two glasses of milk every day.
6. Drinking a glass of warm milk before going to bed at night is good for your health.
7. We must drink plenty of water.
8. We must not waste food.
9. We must not eat food kept uncovered in roadside stalls. Flies and dust settle on uncovered food and contaminate the food. You may fall sick if you eat uncovered food sold by vendors.

Do you know?
Exercises and yoga build strong muscles and bones. Children must play outdoor games like football, volleyball, cricket, tennis, skipping, or participate in any such physical activity every day.

Healthy Teeth

We must brush our teeth in the morning after we wake up and at night before going to bed. It helps to keep teeth clean and strong.

We should not eat too many sweets or chocolates. After we eat sweets or chocolate, we must rinse our mouth well. Excess of chocolate, ice cream, fried foods like chips, burgers, samosas, and cola are bad for our teeth and our health.

We must get our teeth checked by a dentist regularly. We should also visit the dentist if we get toothaches or any other tooth problem like bleeding gums.

The following food items are bad for our teeth:

  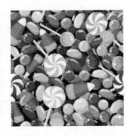

Multiple Choice Questions

1. **Which of these food items helps us to grow**

   A.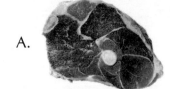

   B.

   C.

   D.

2. **This food is categorized as "protective food"?**

   A.

   B.

   C.

   D.

3. **This food item is a rich source of carbohydrates:**
   A. Cauliflower   B. Fish
   C. Rice   D. Eggs

4. **To be able to do more work, we need:**
   A. Energy   B. Vitamins
   C. Water   D. Protein

5. **What will happen if we do not eat proteins?**
   A. We will not have energy to work
   B. We will not grow well
   C. We will become healthy
   D. We will become weak and not grow well

6. **Which category includes sugarcane?**
   A. Energy giving
   B. Body building
   C. Protective
   D. Both B and C

7. **Which is the richest source of good-quality protein?**
   A. Pulses
   B. Cereals
   C. Egg
   D. Meat

8. **Iron is a:**
   A. Carbohydrate
   B. Mineral
   C. Protein
   D. Vitamin

9. **Fruits are rich in:**
   A. Minerals
   B. Proteins
   C. Vitamins and mineral
   D. Carbohydrates

10. **If you need to replace milk in your diet you should choose which of the following?**
    A. Cereals
    B. Leafy vegetables
    C. Pulses
    D. Cheeses

11. **For good-quality protein, which of the following should be your choice?**
    A. Apples
    B. Eggs
    C. Spinach
    D. Cabbage

12. **Which of the following foods have all the essential nutrients?**
    A. Butter
    B. Eggs
    C. Meat
    D. Pulses

13. **Potatoes are a rich source of:**
    A. Body-building materials
    B. Energy-providing materials
    C. Protective materials
    D. All nutrients

14. **A food item that provides only energy is:**
    A. Bajra
    b. Rice
    C. Sugar
    d. Wheat

15. **Spices help to make food taste good. Which of these is not a spice?**
    A. Raisin
    B. Cinnamon
    C. Turmeric
    D. Chillies

16. **Which of these minerals make our bone strong?**
   - A. Calcium
   - B. Iron
   - C. Chlorine
   - D. Sodium

17. **Which of the following is a bad habit?**
   - A. Eating a variety of food items
   - B. Exercising regularly
   - C. Swallowing the food without chewing
   - D. Drinking a lot of water

18. **Fats and carbohydrates are together called:**
   - A. Protective foods
   - B. Body-building food
   - C. Junk food
   - D. Energy giving food

19. **Sahil should not eat which of the following:**

   A.

   B.

   C.

   D.

20. **We should not skip this meal because the body requires it the most after hours of gap between meals. Which meal are we referring to?**
   - A. Dinner
   - B. Lunch
   - C. Breakfast
   - D. Supper

21. **Why is fish kept in ice as shown in the given image:**

A. It tastes good
B. It cooks well
C. It stays fresh for a longer time
D. Its nutritional value is increased

22. **Select the odd one out:**
    A. Walnut   B. Raisin
    C. Grapes   D. Almonds

23. **Rice is mostly eaten in southern and eastern India. It is termed as:**
    A. Staple food   B. Balanced food
    C. Junk food   D. Breakfast food

24. **We should have one energy-giving food, one protective food, and one body-building food in every meal. Which combination out of the following options is the best?**
    A. Rice, dal, and curd   B. Soup and bread sticks
    C. Rice, dal, and paneer   D. Chapati, dal, vegetables, and curd

25. **Which of these is used to make a beverage?**

A.

B.

C.

D. Both B and C

Answer Key

1. A	2. C	3. C	4. A	5. B	6. A	7. D	8. B	9. C
10. D	11. B	12. B	13. B	14. C	15. A	16. A	17. C	18. D
19. C	20. C	21. C	22. C	23. A	24. D	25. D		

Housing and Clothing

5

Houses

We need a house to live in. A house gives us shelter. It protects us from rain, heat, storms, and the cold weather. It also protects us from thieves and wild animals. A house gives us safety, pleasure, and comfort.

Test Your Skills

How do you feel when you come back home after a long holiday?

A house in which we live with our family is called a home.

Types of Houses

Houses that last for many years are called permanent houses. Some people who move from one place to another live in temporary houses.

Temporary House

Permanent house

Types of temporary houses:

Tents

Some people like mountaineers and soldiers make tents for camping. Tents are made of canvas (a type of cloth).

Caravans

Some people like nomads move from one place to another. They live in houses on wheels, which are called caravans. They can be parked anywhere, just like a car. People who live in caravans are called gypsies.

Houseboat

In Kashmir, people make floating houses on boats. These are called houseboats which float on lake water. When tourists visit Kashmir, they stay in these houseboats for some days for their pleasure.

Dal Lake in Kashmir

Bhemmanad lake in Kerala

Igloos

Special types of houses are built in places which are very cold and covered with ice. They are called igloos. People who live in igloos are called Eskimos.

Did you know?

The early Egyptians used a building material very similar to cement. Romans used a building material obtained by mixing lime and volcanic ash.

Different Kinds of Roofs

There are different types of roofs. Some people make flat roofs on their houses, some make slanting roofs. The type of roof on a house usually depends on the climate of the place.

Slanting roofs are built where it rains or snows heavily. Slanting roofs help rainwater or snow to slide down easily.

Building Materials

Building material is any material which is used for constructing a structure. Many naturally occurring substances, such as clay, sand, wood and rocks, even twigs and leaves have been used to construct buildings. Apart from naturally occurring materials, many man-made products are used for building structures as well.

The different types of building material are:

Wood

Wood is a remarkable and versatile material.

1. Spruce is the light, low-density wood commonly used in house construction.
2. Oak is much heavier, denser, and harder.

Cement

Cement binds the concrete mix together. In the most general sense of the word, cement is a binder, a substance that sets and hardens independently, and can bind other materials together.

Cement

Brick

Bricks are a very important building material. Building brick is usually called "common brick". This is the most frequently used type of brick. It is used for making walls, backing, and other applications where appearance is not important.

House With Concrete Roof   House With Thatched Roof   House With Tinned Roof   House With Clay Tiled Roof

Test Your Skills

Think about different shelters you've seen from around the world. What are the shelters constructed from?

Look at the link below and write a small report on it.
http://www.hgpho.to/wfest/house/house-e.html

Clothes

We wear different clothes in different seasons:

Light, **cotton clothes**, which are capable of absorbing sweat, are mostly worn in summers.

It is very cold in winters. We wear **woollen clothes** in winters to keep ourselves warm.

During the rainy season, we wear **raincoats or carry umbrellas** when we go out. We also wear **gumboots**. They prevent us from getting wet.

Do you know?

The first wool factory in England was established in 50 AD in Winchester by the Romans. In 1797, the British brought 13 Merino sheep to Australia and started the country's Merino sheep industry.

How Clothes are Made?

We get cotton from the pods of cotton plant. This cotton is spun into cotton thread by a process called **spinning**.

This thread is woven into clothes on the loom. This process is called **weaving**. These cotton clothes are used to make different dresses.

We get woollen from the hair of sheep. This hair is cut. It is cleaned and spun into woollen thread. This woollen thread is woven into a woollen cloth or is knitted into caps, gloves, and sweaters.

Cotton, wool, and silk are all natural fibres.

Nylon, rayon, and polyester are man-made fibres.

Multiple Choice Questions

1. **Which of the following is a permanent house?**
   A. Igloo
   B. Tent
   C. Bungalow
   D. Caravans

2. **Which of the following people use temporary houses?**
   A. Soldiers
   B. Scouts
   C. Mountaineers
   D. All of the above

3. **In Kashmir, tourists like to stay in:**
   A. Caravans
   B. Houseboats
   C. Igloos
   D. None of the above

4. **One would find a houseboat in:**
   A. Rajasthan
   B. Uttarakhand
   C. Kashmir
   D. Mumbai

5. **When we need to go out in the rain, we should take an umbrella or wear a:**
   A. Sweater
   B. Raincoat
   C. Scarf
   D. Kurta

6. **Which of the following houses have roof made of straw or palm leaves?**
   A. Tent houses
   B. Caravans
   C. Igloos
   D. Mud houses

7. **Why do houses have sloping roofs?**
   A. To absorb water
   B. To absorb heat
   C. To look beautiful
   D. To help the rain water and snow slip off easily

8. **Houses in the plains have:**
   A. Semi-circular roofs
   B. Curved roofs
   C. Flat roofs
   D. Sloping roofs

9. **Mountain climbers often carry:**
   A. Blocks
   B. Tents
   C. Cardboards
   D. Asbestos sheets

10. **Pucca or permanent houses are built with:**
    A. Bricks, stones, and cement
    B. Cement, grass, and iron rods
    C. Bricks, grass, and water
    D. Stones, cement, and iron rods

11. **Kutcha or temporary houses are built with:**
    A. Bricks, stones, and cement
    B. Mud, grass, and waste material
    C. Bricks, grass, and water
    D. Stones, cement, and iron rods

12. **The following image shows a house which is built in those places where:**

    A. Wind blows very fast
    B. It rains heavily
    C. Climatic conditions are very cold
    D. Heat of the Sun is extreme

13. **It is important to put a wire mesh on doors and windows because:**
    A. It keeps the house warm and dark
    B. It allows sunlight and air to come in
    C. It stops the entry of mosquitoes and flies
    D. B and C both

14. **Which of these kinds of houses are famous in Japan?**
    A. Built of paper
    B. Built of wood
    C. Built of wood and paper
    D. Built of cement

15. **Which of the following gives fibres used to make a sweater?**
    A. Sheep   B. Cocoon
    C. Deer   D. Plants

16. **Which of the following gives fibres used to make a silk sari?**
    A. Sheep   B. Silk worm
    C. Deer   D. Plants

17. **Clothes are made from:**
    A. Worms   B. Plants
    C. Animals   D. Fibres

18. **We wear different clothes. This depends on:**
    A. Type of season
    B. Type of climate
    C. Type of occasion
    D. All of the above

19. **We wear cotton clothes mostly in:**
    A. Rainy season
    B. Winter season
    C. Summer season
    D. None of the above

20. **Which of the following will least absorb sweat?**
    A. Cotton clothes   B. Nylon socks
    C. Silk sari   D. Sweaters

21. **On a sunny day, when we spread wet clothes on a clothesline for drying under the Sun, the following observing points can be extracted:**

    Which of the following statement is/are correct?
    A. Silk clothes absorb the most water
    B. Cotton clothes are heaviest among other fabric clothes
    C. Woollen clothes take the longest time to dry
    D. A and B both

22. **A raincoat is made up of:**
    A. Plastic
    B. A fabric that repels water
    C. A fabric that is water proof
    D. All of the above

23. **Select the incorrect statement from the statements given below:**
    A. Woollen clothes keep us warm
    B. Woollen clothes absorb sweat from our body
    C. Cotton clothes keeps us cool
    D. Synthetic clothes are good to wear in winters

24. **Woollen clothes are made by which process?**
    A. Weaving   B. Wearing
    C. Knitting   D. Spinning

25. **Gandhi ji use to wear:**
    A. Cotton clothes   B. Khadi clothes
    C. Synthetic clothes   D. Silk clothes

Answer Key

1. C	2. D	3. B	4. C	5. B	6. D	7. D	8. C	9. B
10. A	11. B	12. B	13. C	14. C	15. A	16. B	17. D	18. D
19. C	20. B	21. D	22. D	23. B	24. C	25. B		

Family and Festivals, Occupations

6

Learning milestones:
- ☐ Family
- ☐ Types of families
  - ☐ Small family
  - ☐ Big family
- ☐ Family tree

Family

Family is universal and typically consists of a married man and woman, and their children.

Take a look around. You will find that people generally do not live by themselves. They live in families. Even you live in a family. And it is not just in India that we live in families. This is the case everywhere. In other words, it is found in all societies, all over the world.

Big Joint Family

Nuclear family

Do you know?

An ancestor is a parent or grandparent or great grandparent and so on. A child can resemble any of his ancestors.

Types of Families

Families can be categorised as:

I.   Category 1: Small and big family

II. Category 2: Nuclear and joint family

I. Category 1

Small Family

A family is said to be a **small family** if it has a mother, father, and one or two children.

Big Family

A family is said to be **big family** if it has a mother, father, and more than two children.

II. Category 2

The nuclear family

A **nuclear family** comprises of mother, father, and their children only. It does not have grandparents, uncle, and aunt.

Our parents love us. We can make our parents happy by:

♦ Obeying them

♦ Helping them in small household chores like laying the table and watering the plants

Our parents take care of us. They take care of all our needs. They go to office and also take care of the house and children at home.

The joint family

A joint family has parents, children, grandparents, uncles, aunts, and cousins living together.

Your mother's mother or father's mother is your grandmother. Similarly, your father's father or mother's father is your grandfather. Your father's sister or mother's sister is your aunt. Your father's brother or mother's brother is your uncle. Your uncle and aunt's children are your cousins.

We should listen to the advice given by our grandparents. We should spend some time with our grandparents and help them do small tasks that they are unable to do.

Family Tree

A family tree is a diagrammatic representation of family members. Here family members are shown with respect to their relations.

A simple family tree includes grandparents (generally father's parents), their children, and their grandchildren.

Look at the picture of the family tree above. What do you see in it? Write it down.

1. ....
2. ....

Test Your Skills

Play a jumble word game:

Make jumbled word cards with the words given below. Solve the jumble. Now place those words according to relation on a family tree, constructed on a big chart paper. There can be word jumbles which have no relation with the family tree. Sort them out.

A A R D G R F H E N T	
A O R D G R M H E N T	
A A P N J	
I D N A I	
T E R O M H	
E U C L N	
N O C U I S	
R T H F A E	
N T U A	
R B O H R T E	
R T S S I E	

Our Festivals

We celebrate many festivals in India. We have fun during festivals. India is called the land of festivals as many festivals are celebrated in our country.

Some festivals are celebrated by the whole nation. These are called National Festivals.

National Festivals

Independence Day (15th August), Republic Day (26th January), and Gandhi Jayanti (2nd October) are our National Festivals.

1. India got freedom on **15th August, 1947**. Our Prime Minister hoists the national flag at the **Red Fort** in Delhi and addresses the nation on this day.

2. We celebrate **26th January** as our **Republic Day** every year. On this day the national flag is hoisted all over the country.

3. We celebrate **Gandhi Jayanti** on **2nd October** every year. It is the birth anniversary of Mahatma Gandhi.

Religious Festivals

1. **Holi** is also known as the festival of colours. People celebrate this festival by applying colours on each other.

2. **Diwali** is an important festival of Hindus. It is the festival of lights. People clean and decorate their homes on this day. On Diwali night, people light lamps and diyas. People also worship **Goddess Lakshmi** and **Lord Ganesha** on this day.

3. **Christmas** is the main festival of Christians. It is celebrated on 25th December every year. It celebrates the birth of Jesus Christ. People go to the church and sing hymns.

4. **Eid** is the main festival of Muslims. It is celebrated on the last day of Ramzan month. People fast during this month. On Eid, they go to offer namaz in the mosques.

5. **Gurupurav** marks the birthdays of the ten Sikh gurus. The Sikhs go to pray in Gurudwaras on this day. They take out religious and colourful processions.

Different Occupations

Different people do different work. They work to earn money. The work they do is their occupation. The following are some of the occupations people have:

1. A milkman brings us milk.

2. A chemist sells medicines.

3. A barber cuts and trims our hair.

4. A farmer grows food grains.

5. A gardener looks after the plants in the garden.
6. A carpenter makes furniture and other things of wood.

7. A plumber fits and repairs the taps and water pipes.

8. A mason builds houses.
9. A tailor stitches clothes.

10. A cobbler makes and mends shoes.
11. A blacksmith makes things of iron.
12. A postman brings our letters and parcels.

13. Soldiers protect the country from enemies.
14. A doctor treats us when we are ill.
15. A teacher teaches in a school.

Multiple Choice Questions

1. **Ram and Gauri live with their mother and father in Delhi. What type of family is this?**
   A. Small family
   B. Big family
   C. Joint family
   D. Small or nuclear family

2. **Our great grandfathers are called:**
   A. Ancestors
   B. Early man
   C. Old man
   D. Hominids

3. **Early man is called:**
   A. Hominids
   B. Apes
   C. Hunters and gatherers
   D. Stone age man

4. **Sharing and caring involves:**
   A. Taking care of grandparents
   B. Sharing a meal with brothers and sisters
   C. Helping younger brothers and/sisters in their work
   D. All of these

5. **Which of these is not a family occasion?**
   A. Lakshmi puja
   B. Langar
   C. Wedding
   D. Birthday

6. **Which of these is a part of recreation but our parents suggest that we should avoid it?**
   A. Listening to music
   B. Watching TV
   C. Watching TV for a long time
   D. Practising yoga

7. **Traits are:**
   A. Resembling habits
   B. Resembling physical characteristics
   C. Resembling genes
   D. All of the above

8. **How many generations are included when you use the term *grand* as prefix of father, with respect to you?**
   A. 1
   B. 2
   C. 3
   D. 4

9. **You can resemble in traits with your:**
   A. Cousin
   B. Uncle
   C. Grandmother
   D. All of them

10. **One family tree spreads into _____ families:**
   A. 2
   B. 3
   C. 4
   D. Many

11. **Match the following**
   a. Green-grocer   i.   baked bread
   b. Chemist   ii. flies an aeroplane
   c. Baker   iii. sell medicine
   d. Magician   iv. sells vegetables
   e. Pilot   v.   shows magic
   A. a-iv, b-iii, c-i, d-v, e-ii
   B. a-iv, b-iii, c-i, d-ii, e-v
   C. a-iv, b-i, c-iii, d-v, e-i
   D. a-iii, b-iv, c-i, d-v, e-i

12. **Shikha got married to Chander. Chander is Shikha's _____.**
   A. Fiancé
   B. Spouse
   C. Husband
   D. B and C both

13. **Mahatma Gandhi is also called the father of the nation. People go to his *samadhi* at _____, _____ to pay their respects.**
   A. Raj Ghat, New Delhi
   B. New Delhi, Raj Ghat
   C. Raj Ghat, Bhopal
   D. Mumbai, Raj Ghat

14. **Dr Sarvepalli Radhakhrishnan's birthday is celebrated as:**
   A. Children's Day
   B. Father's day
   C. Teacher's Day
   D. None of the above

15. **Chacha Nehru's birthday is celebrated as:**
   A. Children's Day
   B. Father's day
   C. Teacher's Day
   D. None of the above

16. **What is the prayer of Muslims called?**
   A. Aarti
   B. Bhajan
   C. Prayer
   D. Namaz

17. **On this day Hindus do Lakshmi puja at home:**

    A. Holi

    B. Onam

    C. Diwali

    D. Gurupurab

18. **A Langar is organized on this day, where everyone gets free food. Name the festival.**

    A. Diwali

    B. Onam

    C. Lohri

    D. Gurupurab

19. **Name the harvest festival of Kerala.**

    A. Pongal

    B. Onam

    C. Lohri

    D. Holi

20. **Name the harvest festival of Tamil Nadu.**

    A. Pongal

    B. Onam

    C. Lohri

    D. Holi

21. **Which of the following festivals is celebrated on the same day every year?**

    A. Janmashtmi

    B. Christmas

    C. Rakshabandhan

    D. Diwali

22. **He was the first Guru of the Sikh's:**

    A. Guru Arjan Singh

    B. Guru Govind Singh

    C. Guru Nanak

    D. Guru Teg Bahadur

23. **Which of the following festivals is celebrated in the spring season?**

    A. Teej

    B. Dussehra

    C. Raksha bandhan

    D. Holi

24. **This/These festival(s) is/are celebrated by Christians:**

    A. Good Friday

    B. Eid-ul Fiter

    C. Easter

    D. A and C both

25. **Eid is celebrated by:**

    A. Hindus

    B. Muslims

    C. Christians

    D. Sikhs

26. **Name the person who mends our shoes.**

    A. Florist

    B. Cobbler

    C. Grocer

    D. Barber

27. **What does a soldier do?**
    A. Cuts and trims our hair
    B. Grows food grains
    C. Protect the country from enemies
    D. Builds houses

28. **We take help from him when we need flowers to gift someone?**
    A. Postman   B. Florist
    C. Mason   D. Plumber

29. **Ananya's tap is not working properly, she should call a _____.**
    A. Postman   B. Florist
    C. Mason   D. Plumber

30. **The bed in which you sleep is made by:**
    A. Postman   B. Carpenter
    C. Mason   D. Plumber

Answer Key

1. D	2. A	3. A	4. D	5. B	6. C	7. B	8. C	9. D
10. D	11. A	12. D	13. A	14. C	15. A	16. D	17. C	18. D
19. B	20. A	21. B	22. C	23. D	24. D	25. B	26. B	27. C
28. B	29. D	30. B						

Transport and Communication

7

Learning milestones:
☐ Transportation
  ☐ Public and private transport
☐ Communication
  ☐ Early modes of communication
  ☐ Advanced modes of communication
☐ Safety rules
  ☐ Safety rules on the road
  ☐ Safety at home
  ☐ Safety in the school
  ☐ Other safety rules

Transportation

We travel from one place to another. It can be from our house to school or from our house to our relative's place. The mode of travelling we use, to get from one place to the other is called **transportation**.

Means of transport can be fast and slow.

Do you know?

Ferdinand Verbiest invented the first car in the year 1672. It was the first ever car invented and was powered by steam. Ferdinand was an experimentalist and a missionary to China. He built his car in China.

Modes of transport can be further divided into categories like public and private transport.

Private and Public Transport

Private transport is any transport service which is not open to all. This means only people who are related to the owner can travel in it. It is owned or operated by an individual or a group.

Some examples of private transport are bicycle, motor bike, and car.

Public transport is that mode of transport in which anyone can travel. It is generally owned by the government or a company. The passengers are charged money to travel by public transport.

Some of the public transports are city bus, school bus, train, and aeroplane.

Test Your Skills

Look at the following pictures. Identify them and then fill up their names in suitable categories. A mode of transport can also fall into two categories.

Public	Private
Slow	Slow
Fast	Fast

Communication

Communication involves sending and receiving messages. People communicate in different ways.

Early Modes of Communication

Very long ago, people used to communicate with the other people living far away with the help of pigeons. When human beings started taming animals, they used to ride on horse backs to carry messages. In the villages, people used to communicate with the help of drum beats.

Advanced Modes of Communication

1. After inventions of advanced transportation modes, communication became faster and easier. Communication via postal services like letters, inlands, and telegram came into use.

2. Invention of the telephone improved the way of communication and speed of communication.

Do you know?

To call a person within a country we use STD facility (Subscriber Trunk Dialing) and to call a person overseas we use ISD (International Subscriber Dialing) facility.

---

3. Latest modes of communication: The latest modes of communication are via the Internet. The Internet helps us in sending and receiving long messages around the world, almost instantly.

Safety

We must follow some safety rules on the road to be safe.

Safety means protecting ourselves from an accident. Safety habits are for our betterment. They save us from injuries, so it is important that we follow them.

Safety Rules on the Road

1. Walk on the foot path.

2. Cross the road at the zebra crossing.

3. Roads are not safe places to play. So do not play on or near the roads.

4. Cross the road only when the light is red for the traffic.
5. When you cross the road, look to the right, then to the left, and again to the right before crossing.

6. Do not get on a moving bus.
7. Make a queue while boarding a bus.

8. Do not stick your head or hands out of a moving vehicle.

9. Always wait for the traffic to move away before crossing the road.
10. Use the door at the footpath side to get in and out of the car.
11. Small children should always hold an adult's hand while crossing the road and walking to and from school.
12. Wear a correctly fitting helmet when riding your cycle, scooter, or skates. Children must can wear safety gears while riding.

Test Your Skills
Look at the following traffic symbols carefully.

Where have you seen them?

Safety at Home
The following are some safety measures we must follow at home:
1. Do not touch an electrical point with wet hands.
2. Do not play outdoor games inside the house.

3. Do not play with sharp objects or fire.
4. Do not scatter your things on the floor. You may trip and fall.
5. Never run up and down the stairs. You may fall down and hurt yourself.

Safety in the School

The following are some safety measures we must follow in school:

1. Do not run up or down the stairs.
2. Do not jump on the benches.
3. Do not push others.
4. Do not play outdoor games in the class.
5. Do not spill water.

Other Safety Rules

The following are some more safety measures we must follow:

1. Always go for swimming with an adult.
2. Do not tease stray animals.
3. Always play fairly. Do not fight while playing.

First-Aid:

In spite of being careful, we and our friends may get hurt sometimes. In such a situation, contact your elders.

Give some help to the injured person. Immediate help given to an injured person is called First Aid.

Multiple Choice Questions

1. Animal carts like bullock cart, horse cart (tonga), cycles, and large sea ships are examples of:
   A. Fast transport
   B. Slow transport
   C. Public transport
   D. Private transport

2. Which of these can further be divided into categories like public and private transport?
   A. Modes of transport
   B. Means of communication
   C. Slow transport
   D. Fast transport

3. Bicycle, motor bike, and car are examples of:
   A. Public transport
   B. Private transport
   C. Fast transport
   D. Slow transport

4. Pigeons are an example of:
   A. Modern mode of communication
   B. Early mode of communication
   C. Slow mode of communication
   D. Both B and C

5. Which of the following improved the way of communication?
   A. Invention of telephone
   B. Invention of television
   C. Invention of radio
   D. All of the above

6. Latest modes of communication is/are:
   A. Telephone
   B. Telegram
   C. Mobile
   D. A and C both

7. We should cross the road only when the traffic light is:
   A. Blue for the traffic
   B. Red for the traffic
   C. Yellow for the traffic
   D. Green for the traffic

8. When you cross the road:
   A. Look to the left, then to the right, and again to the right before crossing
   B. Look to the left and then to the right before crossing
   C. Look to the right, then to the left, and again to the right before crossing
   D. Look to the right and cross the road

9. Which of the followings is the most expensive means of transport?

A.

B.

C.

D.

10. Which of the following modes of transportation can be run by a gas engine?

A.

B.

C.

D. A and B both

11. **Which of the following modes of transport is run by manpower?**
   A. Bicycle
   B. Bus
   C. Ship
   D. Auto rickshaw

12. **PIN stands for:**
   A. Postal Index Number
   B. Personal Identification Number
   C. Personal Index Number
   D. Postal Identification Number

13. **Distance is measured in:**
   A. Km
   B. Meter
   C. Kg
   D. A and B both

14. **When a traffic police officer signals to stop vehicles, he must approach from the:**
   A. Front side
   B. Behind
   C. Left and right sides
   D. A and B both

15. **Which among the followings likely to be involved in a two-way communication?**
   A. Radio jockey
   B. Editor
   C. Businessman
   D. Manager

16. **Which is the best example of "means of mass communication"?**
   A. Television
   B. Letter
   C. Telephone
   D. Telegram

17. **The below picture signifies:**

   A. Fastest means of communication
   B. E-mail
   C. Slowest means of communication
   D. A and B both

18. **This means of communication carries a message more quickly than a telegram.**
   A. Fax
   B. Letter
   C. Pigeon
   D. None of the above

19. This means of communication was used in the past to send messages faster than letters.

A. Pigeon   B. Telegram

C. Radio   D. Fax

20. Which of the following is an example of auto-visual means of communication?

A. Radio   B. Television

C. Tape recorder   D. Speaker

21. Which of the following is the fastest means of two-way communication?

A. Loudspeaker   B. Emails

C. Telephone   D. Letter

22. The below symbol signifies:

A. Smoking is prohibited here

B. Hospital is straight ahead and near the given place

C. Parking is prohibited here

D. None of the above

23. The below symbols signifies:

A. Red light   B. Pedestrian crossing

C. Zebra crossing   D. B and C both

24. The below icon is for:

A. A telephone   B. A fax machine
C. A telephone booth   D. An e-mail

Answer Key

1.	B	2.	A	3.	B	4.	D	5.	D	6.	D	7.	B	8.	C	9.	C
10.	D	11.	A	12.	A	13.	D	14.	D	15.	A	16.	A	17.	D	18.	A
19.	B	20.	B	21.	C	22.	C	23.	D	24.	B						

Air, Water and Rocks

8

Learning milestones:

- ☐ Air
- ☐ Water
- ☐ Rocks

Air

Air is present all around us. It is important for all living beings. We can neither see, nor touch air. We can only feel air when it moves.

Composition of Air

Air contains water vapour, along with various gases, dust particles, smoke, and germs.

For example: Where does the water from the wet clothes go when we hang them out in the Sun?

1. Water from the clothes changes into water vapour and mixes with the air. Similarly, the heat of the Sun warms up the water in ponds, lakes, and rivers. This water too changes into water vapour and mixes with the air. So, this proves that air contains water vapour.

2. Have you ever seen the little particles when Sun's rays enter into a dark room? These are actually dust particles present in the air. Air picks up dust when it moves.

3. Where do you think the smoke coming out from the big chimneys goes? It mixes with the air, making it impure.

4. There are many germs in the air that can make us ill. Whenever a person sneezes or coughs, the germs are released into the air. These germs can be very harmful for others.

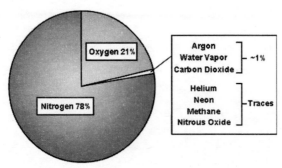

Properties of Air

Air is an essential element for all living beings, just like water. Air is a mixture of many gases like oxygen, nitrogen, carbon dioxide, etc.

Air is a gas. It has no size or shape of its own, but fills every space.

HOTS

Can we see air? Yes/No.

We cannot see air.

We can see or touch water and food but we cannot see or touch air. We can only feel air.

- Blow air from your mouth onto your palm.
- Stand under a moving ceiling fan.
- When you ride your bicycle a little fast, your face and body feels something.
- When you ride a swing and the swing moves fast, you feel something on your face and body again and your clothes and hair blow.

---

1. Air has weight.

Activity

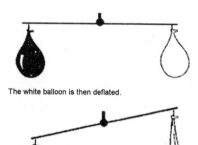

The white balloon is then deflated.

- Take a hanger. Now tie two threads at the two ends of the hanger. Hang the hanger on a nail.
- Now blow up a large balloon.
- Tie its mouth tight. Hang it from one of the threads on the hanger.
- Now tie another balloon, which is not filled with air, on another thread.
- You will now see that the balloon with air sinks down and balloon with no air filled rises.

Explanation: When there is no air in the balloon, the balloon becomes lighter. This suggests that air has weight.

2. Air occupies space and has weight.

When you blow into a balloon, it becomes bigger in size. What is inside the balloon that makes it grow bigger? It is nothing but air. This shows air occupies space and also has weight.

Activity

- Take two handkerchiefs and dip them in water.
- Hang one handkerchief in the hot Sun outside.
- Hang the other in your room.

- After sometime, check both the handkerchiefs.
- You will see that the one you hung outside in the Sun dried faster.
- This is because the heat of the Sun turned the water in the first kerchief into water vapour and the water vapour got mixed into the air.

Clean Air

Plants are our friends. They make the air clean. So we should plant more and more trees around our homes, in parks, and on the roadside.

- We should breathe in fresh and clean air to remain healthy.
- We should keep windows open to let fresh air in.
- We should play out in the open and in green areas to get fresh air.

Moving Air

When the wind blows gently, it is called breeze. Breeze makes us all feel good. When the wind blows fast and is accompanied by rain and thunder, it is called a storm.

A storm can be very harmful as it causes damage to trees, animals, and buildings.

Uses of Wind

1. Wind helps sail boats to move in water.
2. It moves the blades of a windmill which helps to draw ground water and generate electricity.
3. It helps in flying kites.
4. Wind helps clothes to dry.

Water

Water is very important for all living beings. Three fourths of our planet Earth is covered with water. It looks blue from the space. This is the reason why we call earth "The Blue Planet". Water is needed for several daily activities.

We need water for drinking, bathing, cooking, washing, and cleaning.

Water is essential for all living things, plants, and animals. All organisms need water to maintain their life processes. Some organisms live in water, while some others breed only in water.

Sources of water

Rain is the main source of water on Earth. Rain water fills up rivers, streams, lakes, and ponds. This water which we can see on the surface of the Earth is called **surface water**.

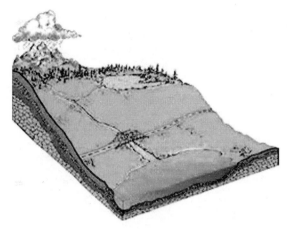

Some rain water seeps into the ground. This water is called **ground water**. Ground water can be dug from wells and pumps.

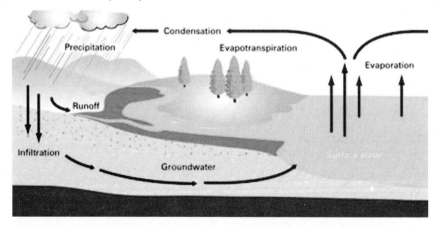

In summers when it is very hot, the water in ponds, rivers, lakes, and seas turns into water vapour and rises into the sky.

Water is also lost from plants and trees as water vapour. The water vapour forms cloud. When clouds cool down, it rains. This is called the **water cycle**.

When it rains, some of the water goes into the soil. It collects deep under the ground. People dig wells and tubewells to bring this water out.

Drinking Water

We get water from taps in our houses.

In towns and big cities, surface and ground water is stored in huge tanks. This water is cleaned in **'water treatment plants'**. After being cleaned, it is sent to various localities through pipes. From these water pipes it reaches our homes.

Tap water may also contain germs, impurities, and mud particles. Drinking dirty water may make us ill. To make it fit for drinking, we should boil and filter it. Boiling water at a high temperature kills the germs.

Once the water is boiled, all the germs in the water are killed and it becomes fit for drinking.

 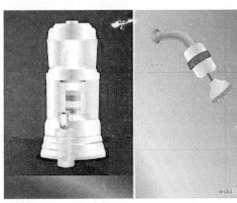

Saving Water

Water should never be wasted. We can save water in many ways:

1. Close taps when not in use.
2. Do not waste water while bathing.
3. Get leaking taps repaired.

NATURAL RESOURCES
Rocks

Rocks are found everywhere on the surface of the earth and even on the sea bed. These are made up of the substances called minerals. The formation of rocks takes millions of years.

> **The scientists who study rocks are called geologists.**

Types of Rocks

Depending on the formation of rocks, they can be classified into three types: Igneous, Sedimentary and Metamorphic.

Igneous Rocks

These are called 'fire rocks' also and are formed from magma. Almost 95% of the earth's crust is made up of igneous rocks. They are formed either under the ground or above the ground. These rocks can further be divided on the basis of minerals they contain.

For example: Granite, obsidian, basalt, pumice

Sedimentary Rocks

While flowing rivers carry sand, soil and pieces of rocks and deposit them into the sea. The carried and heavy materials called sediments sink to the bottom and settle there. The layer after layer of eroded earth gets deposited on each other forming multiple layers. These layers give rise to sedimentary rocks that contain the remains of dead plants and animals collected at the bottom of the sea bed.

For example: Sandstone, conglomerate, limestone, and shale

Metamorphic Rocks

These rocks are formed due to physical and chemical changes in the igneous or sedimentary rocks due to heat and pressure.

For example: Marble, slate, quartzite, and gneiss

Multiple Choice Questions

1. **Air is made up of:**
   A. Liquids
   B. Solids
   C. Gases
   D. All of them

2. **Which of these helps us to fly a kite?**
   A. Wind
   B. Breeze
   C. Air
   D. All of them

3. **Which of these make the air clean?**
   A. Human beings
   B. Green plants
   C. Animals
   D. Factories

4. **When the air is strong and fast, it is called:**
   A. Storm
   B. Breeze
   C. Wind
   D. Air

5. **The air that we breathe in should be:**
   A. Fresh
   B. Warm and dirty
   C. Fresh and cold
   D. Cold and dirty

6. **When water is heated, it changes into:**
   A. Rain
   B. Water vapour
   C. Ice
   D. Smoke

7. **We feel _____ on our face when we run very fast.**
   A. Water vapour
   B. Dust
   C. Air
   D. Smoke

8. **Which is the purest form of water?**
   A. River water
   B. Sea water
   C. Rain water
   D. Pond water

9. **Boiling of water is good because it:**
   A. Purifies the water
   B. Kills the germs
   C. Makes water drinkable
   D. Kills the germs, purifies it, and makes it drinkable

10. **Rain water goes:**
    A. Below the trees roots
    B. Below the soil
    C. Below the ponds
    D. In the sky again

11. **Which statement is completely correct?**
    A. Washing clothes in the river and not supplying waste material from factories into the rivers
    B. Taking domestic animals to the rivers to give them a bath and not throwing domestic garbage into the rivers
    C. Using home pits to burn domestic garbage
    D. Washing clothes in the rivers and throwing waste from factories into the rivers

12. **Which of these instruments is used to check the direction of wind?**
    A. Thermometer
    B. Windmill
    C. Weather cock
    D. Barometer

13. **Which of these has been put under the wrong heading?**

Solid	Liquid	Gas
Molten candle	Lime juice	Water vapour
Eraser	Molten ice	Gas inside the air conditioner

    A. Molten ice
    B. Molten candle
    C. Water vapour
    D. Eraser

14. **The layer of air which surrounds the Earth is called the:**
    A. Atmosphere
    B. Rainfall
    C. Weather
    D. Temperature

15. **Clouds are made up of:**
    A. Water vapour
    B. Steam
    C. Tiny water droplets
    D. Air

16. **Air occupies space and has:**
    A. Force
    B. Temperature
    C. Weight
    D. A and B both

17. **Water can exist in how many states?**
    A. 2
    B. 4
    C. 5
    D. 3

18. **In which form of water can we not see it?**
    A. Solid
    B. Gas
    C. Liquid
    D. Steam

19. **Windmills are used to:**
   A. Grind grains
   B. Pump water
   C. Produce electricity
   D. All of the above

20. **What is evaporation?**
   A. It is the changing of water into water vapour by heating
   B. It is the changing of water into ice by cooling
   C. It is the changing of ice into water by heating
   D. It is the changing of ice into water vapour by heating

21. **Look at the picture given below. It represents:**

   A. Air pollution
   B. Air waves
   C. Storm
   D. Heavy rain with strong wind

22. **Fast and strong winds are called:**
   A. Earthquakes   B. Storm
   C. Wind   D. Breeze

23. **When sunlight passes through water droplets, a _____ is formed in the sky.**
   A. Cloud   B. Pattern
   C. Rainbow   D. Star

24. Which of these activities does not need wind?

A.

B.

C.

D.

25. Which of these do we need to stay alive?
A. Soil B. Water
C. Air D. B and C both

26. When water vapour cools down, it is called:
A. Melting B. Freezing
C. Condensation D. Evaporation

27. Which of these are built to use surface water?
A. Canals B. Wells
C. Dams D. A and C both

28. Which of these pushes the water in the ocean and causes waves?
A. Fishes B. Wind
C. Rocks D. A and B both

29. Which of the following is not a source of surface water?
A. Puddle B. Well
C. Pond D. River

30. Boiling water is not completely pure water because it cannot:
A. Kill the germs
B. Filter the salt present in water
C. Filter the particles present in water
D. B and C both

31. Look at the picture given below.

The lead in pencil is made of:
A. Graphite
B. Granite
C. Sandstone
D. Coal

32. Which of the following rocks is mostly used as tiles on roof?
A. Granite
B. Chalk
C. Coal
D. Slate

33. Match column I with column II and choose the correct option:

Column I	Column II
a. Tungsten	i. Pots and sculptures
b. Graphite	ii. Mirrors
c. China clay	iii. Light bulbs
d. Silica	iv. Pencil lead

A. a-iii, b-iv, c-i, d-ii
B. a-ii, b-iv, c-i, d-iii
C. a-iii, b-i, c-iv, d-ii
D. a-iii, b-iv, c-ii, d-i

34. A soft white rock used to write on the black board is:
A. Quartz
B. Talc
C. Graphite
D. Chalk

Answer Key

1. D 2. D 3. B 4. A 5. A 6. B 7. A 8. C 9. D
10. B 11. C 12. C 13. B 14. A 15. C 16. C 17. D 18. B
19. C 20. A 21. D 22. B 23. C 24. D 25. D 26. C 27. D
28. B 29. B 30. D 31. A 32. A 33. A 34. D

Earth and Universe

Earth and its Structure

Earth's surface is made up of oceans and continents. Continents are landmasses. Most of the Earth is covered by oceans rather than by continents. Over 70 per cent of Earth's surface is water. The surface of Earth's land has different features, such as mountains and valleys.

> **Do you know?**
>
> The Sun has been worshipped as a God. The Sun god was called Ra in Egypt, Helios is Greece, Marduk by the Babylonians, and Utu by the Sumerians.

Landforms

Mountains, plains, plateaus, canyons, and other features are examples of landforms. Landforms are topographic (shape of a given area) features formed by processes that shape Earth's surface.

Plains

Plains are the features that cover most of the Earth. Plains can form from sediments that are deposited by water or wind.

Plateaus

Plateaus, like plains, are flat, but are higher. Plateaus are much higher than the land that surrounds them. Their sides are often steep and rugged. Plateaus are found on every continent, but they are not as common as plains.

Mountains

Mountains are the tallest landforms on Earth. They can form in several ways. Sometimes lava builds up on the ocean floor. Over time, this mound of lava grows tall enough to rise above the ocean's surface. The Hawaiian Islands are mountains that formed in this way.

Search and Find Out
Search and find out the name of three major landform regions in India.

Earth's Rotation – Day and Night

The Earth is a spherical planet. It rotates or spins on its axis.

The word *rotation* means "spinning". This is exactly what the Earth does. It rotates, or spins around, like a top on its axis. It takes 24 hours for the earth to go all the way around. The Earth rotates in an anti-clockwise direction.

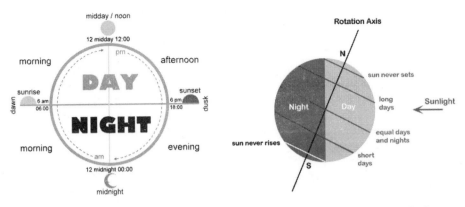

The picture above shows the Earth's rotation and position of the sunlight. Look at the picture carefully. You would see that the side facing the Sun is lighted and the side opposite to the Sun is dark. The 'N' shows where the North Pole is located. Similarly, the 'S' shows where the South Pole is located. The line around the Earth's middle is the equator. The Sun's rays hit the areas around the equator most directly. This means areas by the equator are the warmest. The Sun's rays does not hit the North Pole and the South Pole directly, so the areas here are cold. It can be simply said that the side of the Earth that is the Sun has day and the side of the Earth that is away from the Sun has night.

The Sun

The Sun is a star. It is in the centre of our solar system. The Sun gives us heat and light. Sun is much bigger than the Earth but it looks small because it is far away from us.

The Sun appears to rise in the East and set in the West. It is the main source of energy on the Earth. It is the Sun that makes life possible on Earth. The Sun helps the plants to make their food. This food is eaten by all the living beings. Sunlight kills germs and other disease-causing organisms. The water cycle is also possible because of the Sun.

The Sun and the eight planets (Mercury, Venus, Earth, Mars, Jupiter, Saturn, Uranus and Neptune) that move around it, form our solar system.

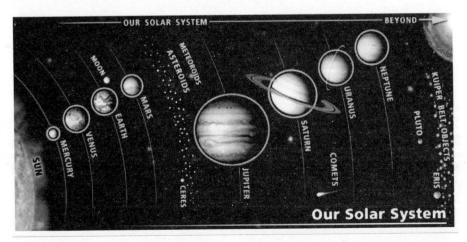

Our Solar System

When the Sun shines we have day, when it sets we have night. At night, we see the Moon and the stars in the sky.

Light and Shadow

Have you ever seen a shadow on the ground? Have you ever thought how a shadow is formed? A shadow is formed when an object blocks the path of light. Only those objects form shadows through which light cannot pass.

Shadows are always formed on the opposite side of the light. If light is coming from the right side, the shadow is formed on the left. If the light is coming from the left side, the shadow is formed on the right. If light is above the object, the shadow will be formed under the object.

Shadows are different in size. They are short at noon and larger in the morning and evening.

Test Your Skills

Can you place the position of Sun in the following figure:
- in the morning at 8 am,
- in afternoon at 12 noon, and
- in evening at 4 pm.

Take care to start from the direction where the word 'East' is written.

National Science Olympiad – Class 2

The Moon

The Moon revolves around the Earth. It is smaller than the Sun and the Earth. The Moon has no light of its own. It shines when the sunlight falls on it. This is the reason why we see different shapes of the Moon every night. There is no life on the Moon as it does not have air and water. The surface of the Moon is rocky.

Just as the Earth revolves around the Sun, the Moon revolves around the Earth. As the Moon revolves around the Earth, it appears to change its shape. These shapes are called **phases of the Moon**.

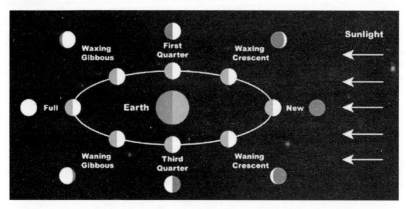

Multiple Choice Questions

1. **The Earth rotates:**
   A. On its axis
   B. Around the Sun
   C. Around the Moon
   D. Around the planets

2. **The Sun helps the Earth by:**
   A. Giving it heat and light
   B. Making plants grow on it
   C. Providing it with food and water
   D. All of these

3. **The shape of a shadow changes according to:**
   A. The movement of the Moon
   B. The size of the object
   C. The movement of the Sun
   D. All of these

4. **The Earth rotates in a _____ path.**
   A. Straight   B. Anti-clockwise
   C. Clockwise   D. Zigzag

5. **_____ Moon is three-fourth lit up.**
   A. Crescent   B. Gibbous
   C. Quarter   D. Full

6. **When there is no Moon, it is called:**
   A. New Moon   B. Full Moon
   C. Crescent Moon   D. Half Moon

7. **Which of the following is not a shape of the Moon?**
   A. Crescent   B. Full Moon
   C. New Moon   D. Waning

8. **Where is a shadow formed?**
   A. Near the source of light
   B. Opposite to the source of light
   C. Both A and B
   D. None of the above

9. **Radium light is a:**
   A. Source of light and indicator
   B. An indicator
   C. A decorator
   D. Symbol of light

10. **Which of the following is not a source of light?**
    A. The Sun
    B. The Moon
    C. Star
    D. Rainbow

11. **Which of these is a star?**
    A. The Moon
    B. The Sun
    C. The Earth
    D. The Venus

12. **How much time does the Earth take to complete one rotation?**
    A. 24 hours
    B. One day
    C. 365 hours
    D. A and C both

13. **A globe is a model of:**
    A. The Sun
    B. The Planet
    C. The Earth
    D. Star

14. **This is the smallest planet in the solar system:**
    A. Venus
    B. Mercury
    C. Earth
    D. Neptune

15. **In the picture below, the planet is revolving around the Sun on its:**

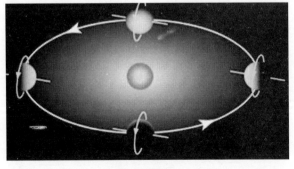

    A. Track
    B. Orbit
    C. Axis
    D. None of the above

16. **What are the major land masses of the Earth called?**
    A. Islands
    B. Continents
    C. Plateaus
    D. Mountains

17. **They are the major water masses on the Earth. They are called:**
    A. Islands
    B. Continents
    C. Oceans
    D. Rivers

18. **An area of fairly level high ground is called:**
    A. Mountain
    B. Plain
    C. Plateau
    D. Continent

19. **Which of these represents the surface of the Earth?**
    A. Plateau
    B. Plain
    C. Landform
    D. All of the above

20. **When we land on the Moon, we:**
    A. Can see earth from there because moon gives its own light
    B. Can see earth from there because earth reflects sunlight
    C. Cannot see earth from there because moon reflects sunlight
    D. Cannot see Earth from there because Earth gives its own light

21. **Which of these is the correct statement?**
    A. The full moon day is called Amavasya
    B. A new moon day is called Purnima
    C. Moon has light of its own
    D. The Sun is a star

22. **Which of these is also called a full-moon day?**
    A. Crescent moon
    B. New moon day
    C. Purnima
    D. Amavasya

23. **How much area of the Earth is covered by water?**
    A. About 1/4th
    B. About 2/3rd
    C. About 3/4th
    D. About 1/2

24. **Identify the figure below. Its shape is:**
    A. Globe, spherical
    B. Globe, round
    C. Globe, flat
    D. Earth, spherical

25. **A full moon has no:**
    A. Shadow on it
    B. Light on it
    C. Shape on it
    D. Phase on it

26. The part of the Moon that looks black or dark, much like the night sky is:

    A. That which is under its own shadow

    B. That which is under the shadow of the Sun

    C. That which is under the shadow of the Earth

    D. Can be any of the above

Answer Key

1. A	2. A	3. C	4. B	5. B	6. A	7. D	8. C	9. A
10. D	11. B	12. D	13. C	14. B	15. B	16. B	17. C	18. C
19. D	20. B	21. D	22. C	23. C	24. A	25. A	26. C	

Section 2
Logical Reasoning

Analogy

Learning milestones:
- ☐ Finding out the relation
- ☐ Finding the missing shape

Analogy means a comparison between two things that have some relationship on the basis of their similarities.

In these types of questions, we have to find out that relation among different options.

Example:

1. Find out the relation.

   Text: Paper: Paper: ?

   A. Pen   B. Book

   C. Ink   D. Pencil

   Hint: As text is found in paper similarly paper is found in book.

2. Find the missing shape by identifying the relationship.

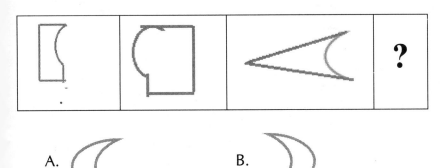

A.    B.

C.   D.

Hint: In the figure, the curved part comes outwards and the pattern is reversed.

Multiple Choice Questions

1. Find out the relation.
   Pen : Ink : : Pencil : ?
   A. Iron   B. Plastic
   C. Graphite   D. Carbon

2. Find out the relation.
   Uttarakhand: Dehradun : : Goa: ?
   A. Patna   B. Panaji
   C. Jaipur   D. Gandhinagar.

3. Find the missing shape by identifying the relationship.

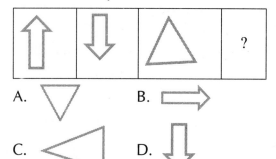

   A. 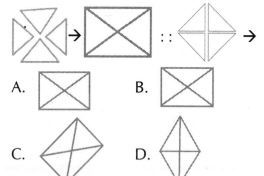 B.

   C.   D.

4. Find the missing shape by identifying the relationship.

   A.   B.

   C.   D.

5. Find out the relation.
   Father : Mother : : Grandfather :?
   A. Grandson
   B. Daughter
   C. Grandmother
   D. Granddaughter

6. Find out the relation.
   Snake : Turtle : : Lizard :?
   A. Cat   B. Fly
   C. Dog   D. Crocodile

7. Find the missing shape by identifying the relationship.

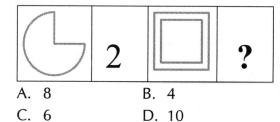

   A. 8   B. 4
   C. 6   D. 10

8. Find the missing shape by identifying the relationship.

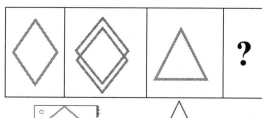

   A. 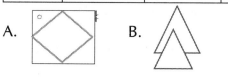   B.

   C.    D.

9. Find the missing shape by identifying the relationship.

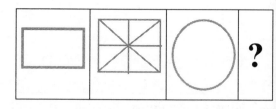

A.   B.

C.   D.

10. Find the missing shape by identifying the relationship.

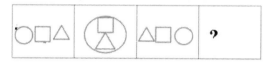

A.   B.

C.   D.

11. Find the missing shape by identifying the relationship.

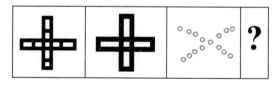

A.   B.

C.   D.

12. Find the missing shape by identifying the relationship.

A.   B.

C.   D.

Choose the word which best completes each analogy for question number 13 to 16.

13. Elbow is to hand as fingers are to
    A. Feet   B. Palm
    C. Leg   D. Body

14. A dolphin is to sea as a chicken is to _____.
    A. Burrow   B. Stable
    C. Hive   D. Coop

15. A week is to 7 days as an hour is to _____ minutes and _____ seconds
    A. 60 min, 60 sec
    B. 100 min, 3600 sec
    C. 60 min, 3600 sec
    D. 3600 min, 60 sec

16. Bark is to tree as skin is to:
    A. Fur   B. Human body
    C. Plastic   D. Vegetables

17. Find the missing shape by identifying the relationship.

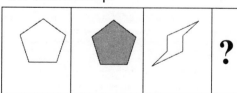

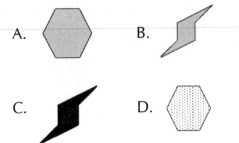

A.   B.

C.   D.

19. Find the missing shape by identifying the relationship.

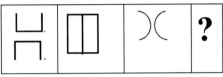

A.   B.

C.   D.

18. Find the missing shape by identifying the relationship.

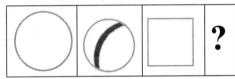

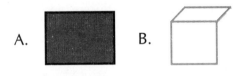

A.   B.

C.   D.

20. Find the missing shape by identifying the relationship.

Guitar; Music; Food:

A. Energy   B. Run

C. Jump   D. Rest

Answer Key

1. C   2. B   3. A   4. D   5. C   6. D   7. A   8. B   9. D
10. A   11. C   12. A   13. B   14. D   15. C   16. B   17. B   18. D
19. B   20. A

Hints and Solutions

1. As Pen needs Ink to write; similarly Pencil needs Graphite.
2. States with capital cities
3. First figure rotates vertically downwards.
4. Joining different parts to form a complete figure
5. As mother is opposite to father; similarly grandmother is opposite to grandfather.
6. Snake, Turtle, Lizard, and Crocodile are reptiles.
7. Counting of straight lines in the figures.
8. Two similar shapes are overlapped on each other.
9. The figures are divided into eight equal parts.
10. The right-most figure enlarges and becomes the outer figure and the second and the third figure gets placed over each other.
11. The half portion of the outer end of the figure is lost.
12. Incomplete letters: Incomplete F → complete F
13. Elbow is the part of hand and fingers are the part of the palm.

Series Completion

2

In this type of test, some numbers or letters are given. They all form a series and change in a certain order. Series has one or more letters or numbers missing. The candidates are required to observe that specific order in which the number or letters would suit the blank space if they continue to change in the same order.

Tips to Solve Series Completion

1. Most series questions are simple with one or two types of modifications in the series, i.e. addition, deletion, rotation or modification. Carefully establish the relationship so that you do not miss an important part.

2. Some patterns are established in only the second consecutive image and others are established only in the third and fourth consecutive images. Work out your pattern from at least three figures to be sure.

3. The most common pattern is rotation which is asked by itself or in addition with other patterns.

4. Do not try to scale the figures, i.e. do not worry about the sizes of lines or shapes unless it is significantly different. There might be drawing errors and there is definitely a much more significant pattern mentioned.

5. As you solve questions, you will come across many patterns. Solving many questions before the exams will help you detect out patterns faster.

6. Figure can move half distance. For example, the figure can move counter-clockwise (clockwise) 1/2, 1 or 1.5 (and so on) sides in each successive figure.

7. When problem figures repeat, use the following tip best applicable when 5 problem figure blocks are given. Compare figure block 1 with 5, if the figure block 5 is identical (or reverse of) figure block 1, the problem figure 2 will be identical (or reverse of) answer figure. This applies to #1 and #4 also in this case #2 will match #5 and #3 will give you the answer figure.

8. When there are many smaller figures in the figure block like, * # @ $ etc. form a matrix and are shifting places and new shapes are replacing old shapes, it may get confusing to deduce the pattern. Use the following approach to simplify the question:

(a) Instead of the shapes, name the smaller figures with digits, i.e. in a 3x3 pattern you can name the positions from 1 to 9.

(b) Begin with elements that are shifting places. Make arrows between positions that are shifting places and put a dot for elements that are not changing positions. Solving for more than one figure block can give you significant insight into the pattern. (c)Now look for new figures replacing the old figure. You must note after how many figures the replacement takes place.

(d) Remember that final position can come in more than one step.

9. Basic clockwise and anti clockwise rotations:

Basic clockwise and anti clockwise rotations

Clockwise rotation   Anticlockwise rotation

10. Basic 45° rotations

11. Basic 90° rotations

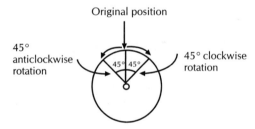

Original position

45° anticlockwise rotation

45° clockwise rotation

12. Basic 180° rotations

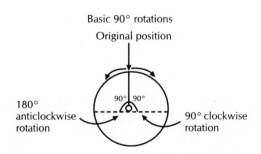

Basic 90° rotations

Original position

180° anticlockwise rotation

90° clockwise rotation

13.

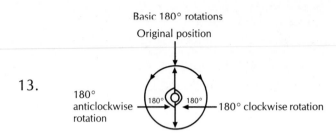

Basic 180° rotations
Original position
180° anticlockwise rotation
180° clockwise rotation

Some important formulas for Series completion:

The sum of the first n natural numbers $= S_n = \dfrac{n(n+1)}{2}$

The sum of the squares of n natural numbers $= \displaystyle\sum_{k=1}^{n} k^2 = \dfrac{n(n+1)(2n+1)}{6}$

The sum of the cubes of the first n natural numbers $= n^3 = \dfrac{n^2(n+1)^2}{4}$

The sum of the first n odd natural numbers $= n^2$

The sum of the first n even numbers $= n(n+1)$

Example

Find the next letter in the series.

B   D   F   H   J   L   ?

    A. N   B. P

    D. O   E. M

       Answer: (A)

Explanation:

The answer is N, because the pattern is to count forward in twos from the first given letter.

B + 2 ➔ D + 2 ➔ F + 2 ➔ H + 2 ➔ J + 2 ➔ L + 2 ➔ N

Example

Find the next pair of letters in the series.

AH   BI   CJ   DK   ?

    A. EL   B. PU

    C. OT   D. MS

       Answer: (A)

Explanation:

The answer is EL, because the pattern is to count forwards in ones for both the fist letter and the second letter.

First letter   AH   BI   CJ   DK   E

Second letter   AH   BI   CJ   DK   EL

Example 3

Find the missing number in the pattern given below.

    2   4   6   8   ?   12

A. 9   B. 10

C. 11   D. 7

    Answer: (B)

Explanation:

$2+2 \rightarrow 4+2 \rightarrow 6+2 \rightarrow 8+2 \rightarrow 10+2 \rightarrow 12$

Multiple Choice Questions

Direction for 1 to 8: Find the next letter in the series given below.

1. C D E F G ?
   A. K   B. J
   C. I   D. H

2. A D G J M ?
   A. O   B. P
   C. Q   D. R

3. D F H J L ?
   A. O   B. N
   C. M   D. P

4. F G H I J ?
   A. N   B. L
   C. K   D. M

5. C E G I K ?
   A. M   B. N
   C. O   D. L

6. Z Y X W V ?
   A. T   B. U
   C. S   D. R

7. P M J G D ?
   A. L   B. B
   C. A   D. Z

8. W V T Q M ?
   A. F   B. G
   C. I   D. H

Direction for 9 to 15: Find the next pair of letters in the series.

9. FA GB HC ID JE ?
   A. GL   B. KF
   C. KG   D. LH

10. WH TJ QL NN KP ?
    A. JR   B. JQ
    C. HS   D. HR

11. HP IR JT KV LX ?
    A. MY   B. MZ
    C. YL   D. NZ

12. KU KT LS LR MQ ?
    A. NP   B. NQ
    C. QM   D. MP

13. HI IH HJ JH ?
    A. GJ   B. HK
    C. JG   D. KH

14. AV BW CX DY ?
    A. DU   B. EZ
    C. FA   D. FZ

15. EZ DY CX BW ?
    A. AV   B. ZU
    C. ZV   D. AU

Direction for 16 to 20: Find the number that continues each sequence in the most sensible way.

16. 9 11 14 18 23 ?
    A. 32   B. 27
    C. 29   D. 36

17. 13 24 35 46 ?
    A. 57   B. 68
    C. 69   D. 67

18. 232 343 454 ?
    A. 545   B. 565
    C. 656   D. 575

19. 10, 100, 200, 310, ?

    A. 400   B. 410

    C. 420   D. 430

20. 11, 10, ?, 100, 1001, 1000, 10001

    A. 101   B. 110

    C. 111   D. None of these

Answer Key

1. D	2. B	3. B	4. C	5. A	6. B	7. C	8. D	9. B
10. D	11. B	12. D	13. D	14. C	15. A	16. C	17. B	18. B
19. D	20. A							

Hints *and* Solutions

1. C($+2$)→D($+2$)→E($+2$)→F($+2$)→G($+2$)→H.
2. A(3)→D($+3$)→G($+3$)→J($+3$)→ M($+3$)→ P.
3. D($+2$)→F($+2$)→H($+2$)→J($+2$)→L($+2$)→N.
4. F($+1$)→G($+1$)→H($+1$)→I($+1$)→J($+1$)→K.
5. C($+2$)→E($+2$)→G($+2$)→I($+2$)→K($+2$)→M.
6. Z(-1)→Y(-1)X(-1)→W(-1)→V(-1)→U.
8. W(-1)V(-2)→T(-3)→Q(-4)→M(-5)→H. Answer is D
16. 9($+2$)11)→($+3$)14($+4$)→18($+5$)→23($+6$)→29.
17. 13($+11$)→2)→35($+11$)→46($+11$)→57($+11$)→68.
18. 232($+111$)→343($+111$)→454($+111$)→565.

Classification

3

Classification (Odd One Out)

Classification test which is popularity known as 'Odd Man Out' test requires assorting of the items of a given group on the basis of a certain common quality they possess and then spotting the odd one in the group.

In this type of questions out of 3-4 objects (may be letters, words, numbers or figures) all but one are similar in some respect. We have to sort out which one is different. (*i.e.*, does not bear the same characteristics as the others in the given group.)

Types of Classification

(i) **Alphabet/Letter Classification :** In this type we have to identify an alphabet or a group of alphabets that are different from other given items.

(ii) Number Classification

(iii) Word Classification

Example 1: Find odd one out.

    (a) N   (b) M   (c) I   (d) E

Solution : **(a)** Except N, any other has odd place value in the English alphabet.

Example 2: Three of the following four are alike in same way and so form a group Which is one that does not belong to that group?

    (a) 37   (b) 48   (c) 59   (d) 38

Solution : **(d)** Except 38, in all other number, difference between two digits is 4.

Multiple Choice Questions

Directions (Q. 1–5) : In each of the following questions choose the one which is different from the others.

1. A. Cow   B. Fish
   C. Goat   D. Cat

2. A. Gold   B. Iron
   C. Diamond   D. Silver

3. A. Ears   B. Hands
   C. Fingers   D. Eyes

4. A. Sun   B. Moon
   C. Venus   D. Earth

5. A. Walk   B. Run
   C. Jog   D. Sit

6. A. April   B. February
   C. November   D. September

7. A. Hand   B. Foot
   C. Chin   D. Cheek

8. A. January   B. December
   C. June   D. August

9. A. 4   B. 8
   C. 16   D. 15

10. A. 9   B. 11
    C. 15   D. 14

11. A. 810   B. 145
    C. 505   D. 235

12. A. 2 : 8   B. 1 : 5
    C. 6 : 24   D. 3 : 12

13. A. A   B. O
    C. U   D. T

14. A. F   B. B
    C. U   D. V

15. A. 37   B. 47
    C. 57   D. 66

Directions (Q. 16–19) : Find out the letter(s) which is different.

16. A. A   B. F
    C. H   D. M

17. A. O   B. S
    C. G   D. T

18. A. AB   B. CD
    C. EF   D. MH

19. A. ABC   B. DEF
    C. GHI   D. ZXY

Answer Key

1. B 2. C 3. C 4. B 5. D 6. B 7. C 8. C 9. D
10. D 11. A 12. B 13. D 14. C 15. D 16. D 17. D 18. D
19. D

Hints *and* Solutions

6.

Months	No. of Days
April	30
February	29
November	30
September	30

7. Except him all other are in pair.

8. Except June, all other months have 31 days each.

9. 15 is an odd number.

11. Except 180, last digit of each number ends with 5.

13. Except T, all other are vowels.

14. Except U, all other are consonants.

Odd One Out

4

Learning milestones:
❏ Identifying the odd object from a group

Odd one out means to point out the component which does not fit in a group. For example, a bird among a group of animals is the odd one.

In these types of questions, we need to identify the odd object or subject among various options.

Example:

1. Choose the odd one out.

   A. Cooler   B. Fan
   C. Air conditioner   D. Water heater

   Solution: Among all the options, option D, water heater is the odd one out, as all the other options provide cooling while water heater is used for heating.

2. There are four figures given below. Choose the odd one out.

   A.   B.

   C.   D.

   Solution: Option C is the odd one out here. All the shapes except the circle has corners.

Multiple Choice Questions

1. Choose the odd one out.
   A.   B.

   C.   D.

2. Choose the odd one out.

   16, 20, 24, 28, 32, 38, 40
   A. 20   B. 28
   C. 33   D. 38

3. Choose the odd one out.
   A. Square   B. Rhombus
   C. Cube   D. Rectangle

4. Choose the odd one out.
   A.   B.

   C.   D.

5. Choose the odd one.
   A.   B.

   C.   D.

6. Choose odd one out.
   A.   B.

   C.   D.

7. Look at the following pictures carefully and choose odd one out.
   A.   B.

   C.   D.

8. Choose odd one out.
   A.   B.

   C.   D.

9. Choose the odd one.

   72, 36, 18, 6, 4.5
   A. 4.5   B. 6
   C. 3   D. 18

10. Choose the odd one.
    A.   B.

    C.   D.

11. Choose odd one out.
    A.   B.

    C.   D.

2. Which of the following alphabet is the odd on the basis of geometrical lines?

A.

B.

C. E

D. W

3. Choose the odd one.
   A. Eye
   B. Radar
   C. Level
   D. Money

4. Choose the odd one.

A.

B.

C.

D.

5. Choose the odd one.

A.

B.

C.

D.

16. Choose odd one out.

A.

B.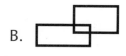

C.

D.

17. Choose the odd one.
    A. E
    B. O
    C. A
    D. T

18. Choose odd one out.
    A. Candy Crush Saga
    B. Tennis
    C. Temple Run
    D. Subway Surfers

19. Choose the odd one.
    A. Knee
    B. Arm
    C. Hand
    D. Fingers

20. Choose the odd one.
    A. Belt
    B. Scarf
    C. Capris
    D. Necklace

Answer Key

1. B 2. D 3. C 4. D 5. B 6. C 7. C 8. C 9. B
10. A 11. D 12. B 13. D 14. C 15. C 16. A 17. D 18. B
19. A 20. D

Hints and Solutions

1. Except B all the other options have a smaller shape inserted into a bigger shape.
2. Add 4 to each number.4.
3. Option C has six sides whereas shapes in the other options have four sides.
4. Option D is not a manually-played musical instrument.
5. A is healthy food whereas rest is all junk food.
6. C, Figure A, B and D are divided into four parts equally except figure C which is divided into three parts.
7. A, B and D provide us milk, but not C.
8. A, B and D are overlapping shapes whereas in option C the pattern is different with no overlapping.
9. Divide each number by 2 to get the next number in the series.
10. B, C and D smileys have three circles and 1 curve in each but in smiley A there are three circles and three curved lines.
11. In figure A, B and C, alternate circles are coloured
12. A, C and D are formed by straight lines, whereas B is formed from a curved line.
13. D, Because it is not the same when spelt backwards.
14. A, B and D are fruits, C is a vegetable
15. **Hint:** Except C, all are indoor games.
16. Other than figure A, all the figures intersect.
17. Option A, B and C are vowels
18. Except B all the other options are mobile games.
19. B, C and D, all belong to upper limb.
20. Other than option D, all the options are of clothes.

Coding and Decoding

5

Learning milestones:
- ☐ Letter to letter
- ☐ Letter to number
- ☐ Miscellaneous types

Coding-decoding is a signal system which is used in conveying the messages by using certain codes to represent letters or numbers. It is a web of symbols, letters or words. For example, If a glass is coded as "drink", it will be called as a drink only.

There are three main types of coding-decoding categories. They are

    A. Letter to letter

    B. Letter to number

    C. Miscellaneous types

For example,

1. If GIVE is written as EVIG, OVER is written as REVO, then how will 'DISK' be written in that same code?

    A. SIDK   B. KISD

    C. KIDS   D. KSID

Hint: Reverse the alphabet.

1. G = 4. E	1. O = 4. R	1. D = 4. K
2. I = 3. V	2. V = 3. E	2. I = 3. S
3. V = 2. I	3. E = 2. V	3. S = 2. I
4. E = 1. G	4. R = 1. O	4. K = 1. D

2. If BAT is coded as = 23, then EAGLE is coded as _____

    A. 26   B. 30

    C. 36   D. 20

Hint: As A = 1, B = 2, C = 3 and so on, then,

B A T = 1 + 2 + 20 = 23

Similarly, E A G L E = 5 + 1 + 7 + 12 + 5 = 30

3. A curtain has three colours: red, white and black, If red is called white, white is called black, black is called green. Then which colour is on the last strip of the curtain?

    A. Green   B. Black

    C. Red   D. White

Hint: Last strip on the curtain is of black colour and black is called green.

Multiple Choice Questions

Alphabet in natural series are

A=1	B=2	C=3	D=4	E=5	F=6	G=7	H=8	I=9	J=10
K=11	L=12	M=13	N=14	O=15	P=16	Q=17	R=18	S=19	T=20
U=21	V=22	W=23	X=24	Y=25	Z=26				

Directions (1–3)

1. If TABLE is written as 40, then CHAIR will be written as _____
   A. 39
   B. 38
   C. 26
   D. 36

2. If CARROT = 75, then RADDISH will be written as _____
   A. 76
   B. 36
   C. 63
   D. 85

3. If SEA = 13, then YAK will be written as _____
   A. 16
   B. 13
   C. 17
   D. 8

Directions (4–5)

4. If HELP is coded as 8-5-12-16, then how will you code HORSE?
   A. 8-18-19-15-5
   B. 8-15-5-19-18
   C. 8-15-18-19-5
   D. 8-19-15-5-18

5. If GOAT is coded as 7-15-1-20, then how will you code SHEEP?
   A. 19-13-5-5-16
   B. 19-8-5-5-16
   C. 19-15-5-5-8
   D. 19-8-5-5-16

Directions (6–12)

6. If house is called nest, nest is called hole, hole is called den, then in which place do birds live?
   A. Den
   B. Hole
   C. Nest
   D. House

7. If grass is called insects, insects are called birds, birds are called owl, then what is the name of the insects?
   A. Grass
   B. insects
   C. owl
   D. Birds

8. If tiger is called lion, lion is called elephant, elephant is called bear, then who is the king of jungle?
   A. Tiger
   B. Lion
   C. Bear
   D. Elephant

If night is called evening, evening is called day, day is called morning, morning is called night, then answer the following questions (9–10):

9. What is the time for sunset?
   A. Day
   B. Morning
   C. Evening
   D. Night

10. When do we wake up?
    A. Morning
    B. Day
    C. Evening
    D. Night

11. If January is called February, February is called March, March is called April, April is called January, then which of these is called fourth month of the Year?
    A. February
    B. April
    C. January
    D. March

12. If Sun is called Moon, Moon is called Earth, Earth is called Mars, Mars is called Sun, then we live on _____
    A. Mars
    B. Earth
    C. Moon
    D. Sun

13. If ◇ can be written as 4, ○ can be written as 0, △ can be written as 3, th ⬡ can be written as _____

A. 4   B. 6
C. 5   D. 3

14. In a certain code, HORSE is written as PMNBY and CAMEL is written as LOQYK. How will HARE be written in that same code?
A. PONY   B. PLOY
C. OPNY   D. NYOP

Direction (15–16)

15. In a certain code language, CAT is written as XZG. How will TEA be written in that same code language?
A. VZG   B. ZGV
C. GVZ   D. GZV

16. In a certain code language, DOLL is written as WLOO. How will TEDDY be written in that same code?
A. GVWVB   B. WGBVW
C. GVWWB   D. GWWVB

Direction (17–18)

17. If MIRROR is coded as RORRIM, then CAMERA will be codedas?
A. AREMAC   B. ARECAM
C. AREMCA   D. AREAMC

18. If DOORMAT is coded as TAMROOD, then REFRIGERATOR will be coded as _____
A. ROTAREGERFRI
B. ROTAREGIRFER
C. ROTAREGIRRFE
D. ROTAREGIRFRE

Direction (19–20)

19. If '853' is coded '631', '974' is coded '752', then '594' is coded as _____
A. 327   B. 632
C. 532   D. 372

20. If '2961' is coded '1850, '3854' is coded '2743, then '1539' is coded as _____
A. 4860   B. 0428
C. 4806   D. 0529

Answer Key

1. C 2. B 3. A 4. D 5. C 6. D 7. A 8. B 9. D
10. A 11. C 12. A 13. B 14. D 15. C 16. B 17. B 18. D
19. B 20. A

Hints and Solutions

1. As, T A B L E $= 20+1+2+12+5 = 40$
   Similarly, C H A I R $= 3+8+1+9+18 = 39$

2. As C A R R O T $= 3+1+18+18+15+20 = 75$ Similarly, R A D D I S H
   $= 18+1+4+4+9+19+8 = 63$

3. As S E A $= 19-5-1 = 13$
   Similarly, Y A K $= 25-1-11 = 13$

4. As, A $= 1$, B $= 2$, C $= 3$, D $= 4$ and so on.
   Then,
   H $= 8$, E $= 5$, L $= 12$, P $= 16$
   Similarly, H $= 8$, 0 $= 15$, R $= 18$, S $= 19$, E $= 5$

5. As G $= 7$, O $= 15$, A $= 1$, T $= 20$
   Similarly, S $= 19$, H $= 8$, E $= 5$, E $= 5$, P $= 16$

6. Birds live in nest, but nest is called hole.

7. Grass is called insects, but insects are called as birds.

8. The king of jungle is Lion and Lion is Elephant.

9. The time of sunset is Evening but here Evening is called Day.

10. We wake up in morning but here morning is called night.

11. Fourth month of the year is April, but April is called January.

12. We live on Earth and Earth is called Mars.

13. Number of straight lines in ⬨ $= 4$

    Number of straight lines in ◯ $= 0$

    Number of straight lines in △ $= 3$

Number of straight lines in ⬡ = 6

14. Using the letter code

H	P		C	L
O	M		A	O
R	N		M	Q
S	B		E	Y
E	Y		L	K

Similarly, from these codes, we get

H	P
A	O
R	N
E	Y

15. Reverse the order of alphabets. i.e., A = Z, B = Y, C = X and so on.

    Hence, C = X A = Z, T = G
    Similarly,
    TEA = GVZ

16. Reverse the order of alphabets. i.e., A = Z, B = Y, C = X and so on.
    Hence, D = W, O = L, L = 0, L = O
    Similarly,
    TEDDY = GVWWB

17. Reverse the alphabets.

18. Reverse the alphabets.

19.

8	5	3	9	7	4
6	3	1	7	5	2

    The numbers are getting deducted by 2 in the code: 8-2 = 6; 5-2 = 3

20. In the code, the original numbers are individually getting deducted by 1. 2-1 = 1
    9-1 = 8, 6-1 = 5, 1-1 = 0, so: 2961 = 1850.

Ranking Test

Learning milestones:
- ❏ Identifying the position or rank of an object or a person
- ❏ Interchanging the positions of two persons or objects
- ❏ Identifying the position of an object with respect to other object
- ❏ Identifying the position or object after removing some objects

Ranking is based on the arrangement of different things like, persons, objects or characters based on some special feature in a specific order.

Ranking test can be of various categories:

1. In the first category, position or rank of an object or a person is identified from left end or right end or from top or bottom.

2. Second category is based on interchanging of the positions of two persons or objects.

3. Third category is based on the position of any person or object with respect to other person or object.

4. Fourth category is based on the identification of position or object after removing some of the objects in the series.

For example,

1. Observe the following figures carefully.

Left   Right

First   Last

a → → b → → c → → d → → e → → f → → g → → h

Apple at the fourth position is the immediate left of the ____ apple.

   A. c   B. e

   C. a   D. f

Solution

d number apple is at the 4th position and it is the immediate left to the e apple.

2. Observe the following figure carefully:

   If Summi's position is interchanged by Somya's postion, then which girl will be positioned at 6th position?

   A. Somya   B. Summi
   C. Somi   D. Sonu

3. If the right most apple is eaten by someone, which apple will become the fifth from the right end?

Left   Right

E   F   O   G   H   P   I   J

   A. H   B. G
   C. O   D. P

Multiple Choice Questions

Direction (1–5): Observe the given figure carefully and answer the following questions.

Left (first)

1. Which bird is seventh from the right end?
   A. M
   B. L
   C. N
   D. P

2. Bird O is second to the right of bird _____.
   A. P
   B. I
   C. M
   D. N

3. If bird P and I interchange their positions, then bird _____ is at the left end.
   A. I
   B. L
   C. P
   D. M

4. Bird J is just left to _____ bird.
   A. N
   B. O
   C. M
   D. L

5. Bird _____ is the sixth bird to the right of bird N.
   A. J
   B. K
   C. M
   D. L

Direction (6–10):

Observe the given figure carefully and answer the following questions.

Left   Right

6. Which umbrella is 10th from the right end?
   A. D
   B. H
   C. J
   D. G

7. If Suhani took the immediate left umbrella of the umbrella K, which umbrella did she take?
   A. M
   B. N
   C. F
   D. H

8. Identify the position of the blue umbrella (from the left) which is just left to red and just right to green umbrellas.
   A. Fifth
   B. Sixth
   C. Ninth
   D. Seventh

9. Umbrella E is _____ to the left of umbrella F.
   A. Second
   B. Fourth
   C. Fifth
   D. Third

10. Umbrella _____ is the right of F and left of L.
    A. K
    B. I
    C. L
    D. G

Direction (11–13): Observe the given figure carefully and answer the following questions.

Left/First

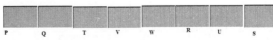

11. W brick is at the 5th position from the left. Now find out the name and position (from the left) of the brick which is at the immediate left of the W brick.
    A. V, fifth
    B. R, fifth
    C. V, fourth
    D. R, fourth

12. If P brick and U brick interchange their position, then brick ____ is at the left end.
   A. Q   B. U
   C. P   D. S

13. Which brick is seventh to the right of brick P?
   A. S   B. U
   C. R   D. P

14. How many threes are there between 10th and 38th tree?
   A. 28   B. 30
   C. 27   D. 20

Direction (15–16)

Observe the given figure carefully and answer the following questions.Left/First

15. Sushma is standing between _____ and _____.
   A. Reema and Ananya
   B. Meghna and Reema
   C. Jyoti and Shiva
   D. Ananya and Shiva

16. If Ananya and Shiva interchange their positions, then Ananya will be at the immediate left of _____.
   A. Reema   B. Jyoti
   C. Meghna   D. Sushma

17. There are 20 students in a class. Six of them are standing, and 10 of them are sitting in the class. Now find out the number of remaining students in the class.
   A. 16   B. 4
   C. 6   D. 8

Direction (18–20): There are 10 rows of students in a class, five students in each row. Rohit is sitting at the 3rd position (from the left) of the fourth row, Sumit is at the 5th position in the same row, and Sneha at the immediate right of Rohit.

18. Where is Sneha sitting?
   A. 6th   B. 10th
   C. 4th   D. 5th

19. On which row, from the back, is Rohit sitting?
   A. 4th   B. 7th
   C. 6th   D. 5th

20. If Rohit is sitting at the 8th position from the front, then what will be his position from the end of the row among 20 students?

Answer Key

1. C	2. B	3. A	4. C	5. D	6. A	7. A	8. A	9. D
10. B	11. C	12. B	13. A	14. C	15. B	16. A	17. B	18. C
19. A	20. B							

Patterns

7

Learning milestones:
- ❏ Finding out the next shape in a series
- ❏ Finding out the next number in a series

You can use patterns to decide what shapes come next in a design. Look at the design and find the repeated pattern.

What are the next three shapes in the pattern?

The pattern is: square, circle, triangle; square, circle, triangle. So the next three shapes in the pattern are:

You can use patterns to decide what numbers come next in a design with a series of numbers. Look at star A. Point number 1 has a value of 4. Go to the next point and look for a number pattern in the star.

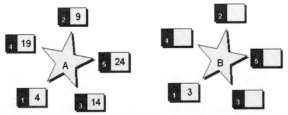

What is the difference between each number? Each number is 5 more than the one before it.

The first point is 4.

The second is 9.

The third is 14.

The fourth is 19.

The fifth is 24.

National Science Olympiad – Class

Use the same number pattern to find the next four numbers in star B. Start with the first point as 3 and add 5 each time to get the next number. They should be 8, 13, 18, 23.

You can use patterns to decide what numbers come next in a series of numbers.

Example:

Look for a number pattern.

2, 5, 8, 11, __, __, __

What is the difference between each number? Each number is 3 more than the one before it. Use the number pattern to find the next three numbers.

11 + 3 = 14   14 + 3 = 17   17 + 3 = 20

→2, 5, 8, 11, 14, 17, 20

Example:

Look for a number pattern.

11, 9, 7, __, __, __,

What is the difference between the numbers? Each number is 2 less than the number before. Use the number pattern to find the next three numbers.

11 – 2 = 9   9 – 2 = 7   7 – 2 = 5   5 – 2 = 3   3 – 2 = 1

11, 9, 7, 5, 3, 1

You can use number patterns to complete a table. The number pattern is the rule for the table.

IN	2	3	4	5	9	10
OUT	5	6	7			

So, what is the rule? What do you have to do to each IN number to get the OUT number below it?

2 + 3 = 5   3 + 3 = 6   4 + 3 = 7

You add 3 to each IN number to get the OUT number. The rule for this table is Add 3. Use the rule to complete the table.

IN	2	3	4	5	9	10
OUT	5	6	7	8	12	13

Find the number pattern to complete the table.

IN	11	10	9	5	7	6
OUT	7	6	5			

Here, you subtract 4 from each IN number to get the OUT number.

11 – 4 = 7   10 – 4 = 6   9 – 4 = 5

The rule for this table is subtract 4.

IN	11	10	9	5	7	6
OUT	7	6	5	1	3	2

Multiple Choice Questions

1. What are the next two shapes to complete the pattern?

   A. circle, circle
   B. Triangle, circle
   C. circle, triangle
   D. Square, circle

2. What are the next two shapes to complete the pattern?

   A. circle, circle
   B. triangle, square
   C. circle, triangle
   D. Square, circle

3. Find the number pattern in star A. The first point has a value of 3. Then look at star B. Use the same number pattern to figure out the value of the other points.

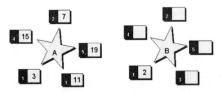

   A. 5, 7, 9, 18
   B. 4, 6, 8, 10
   C. 6, 10, 14, 18
   D. 10, 12, 14, 16

4. What number should be on the other points of star B if you follow the same pattern?

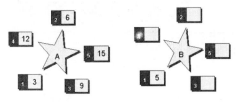

   A. 5, 7, 9, 18
   B. 8, 11, 15, 17
   C. 6, 10, 14, 18
   D. 8, 11, 14, 17

5. Write the next 3 numbers in the pattern.
   30, 32, 34, __, __, __
   A. 36, 38, 40   B. 34, 36, 38
   C. 36, 40, 44   D. None of these

6. Write the next 3 numbers in the pattern.
   5, 10, 15, __, __, __
   A. 25, 30, 35   B. 20, 25, 30
   C. 25, 35, 45   D. 20, 30, 40

7. Write the next 3 numbers in the pattern.
   27, 24, 21, __, __, __
   A. 15, 12, 10   B. 20, 19, 18
   C. 18, 15, 12   D. None of these

8. Write the next 3 numbers in the pattern.
   24, 20, 16, __, __, __
   A. 10, 8, 6   B. 4, 6, 8
   C. 6, 10, 14   D. 12, 8, 4

9. Write the numbers to complete the table given below.

IN	2	3	4	5	8	10
OUT	4	5	6			

   A. 7, 10, 12   B. 4, 6, 8
   C. 6, 10, 14   D. 12, 8, 4

10. Write the numbers to complete the table given below.

IN	4	5	6	7	9	10
OUT	8	9	10			

A. 10, 8, 6   B. 11, 13, 14
C. 6, 10, 14   D. 12, 8, 4

11. Find the letter which will end the first word and start the second word.

   MA?ET

A. K   B. T
C. N   D. L

Directions from 12 to 20 :

In each of the following questions which alternative will replace the question mark.

12. NA is to LF as XN is to?
   A. YS   B. VS
   C. YM   D. WM

13. KM is to OJ as VH is to ?
   A. AG   B. YF
   C. ZE   D. YG

14. GH is to KL as PQ is to?
   A. ST   B. TU
   C. UV   D. UT

15. YW is to VT as NL is to?
   A. IK   B. JH
   C. KI   D. HJ

16. FG is to JK as NO is to?
   A. TU   B. UT
   C. RT   D. RS

17. 4 is to 16 as 16 is to?
   A. 72   B. 64
   C. 60   D. 33

18. 3 is to 12 as 12 is to?
   A. 24   B. 48
   C. 36   D. 25

19. 32 is to 16 as 16 is to?
   A. 4   B. 8
   C. 12   D. 47

20. 22 is to 11 as 24 is to?
   A. 11   B. 12
   C. 14   D. 30

Answer Key

1. A   2. B   3. C   4. D   5. A   6. B   7. C   8. D   9. A
10. B 11. C 12. C 13. D 14. D 15. C 16. C 17. B 18. B
19. B 20. B

Hints and Solutions

2. Here N A $\xrightarrow{+5}$ L F (with -2)   Similarly, X N $\xrightarrow{+5}$ V S (with -2)

5. Here Y W $\xrightarrow{-3}$ V T (with -2, -3)   Similarly, N L $\xrightarrow{-3}$ K I (with -2, -3)

7. Here $4 \rightarrow 4 \times 4 = 16$ Similarly, $16 \rightarrow 16 \times 4 = 64$

9. Here $32 \rightarrow \dfrac{32}{2} = 16$ Similarly, $16 \rightarrow \dfrac{16}{2} = 8$

Problems Based on Figures

8

Pictographs

Pictures that represent information are called pictographs. A pictograph uses pictures or symbols to represent an assigned amount of data. It is a useful method to represent data attractively.

Numerical data when presented through pictures is called pictorial representation.

Pictographs are also called as pictograms.

The picture graph below shows the Groceries Navneet bought for his restaurant in January. Study the graph and answer the given questions.

Groceries Navneet bought in January						
Rice	🛍	🛍	🛍	🛍	🛍	🛍
Sugar	🛍	🛍	🛍			
Flour	🛍	🛍	🛍	🛍		
Barley	🛍	🛍				
Oats	🛍	🛍	🛍			

Each stands for 4 kg.

Example 1 : He bought _____ kg of rice.

A. 16	B. 12
C. 24	D. 8

Solution : **(C)** Navneet bought = 4 × 6 = 24 kg.

Example 2 : He bought 16 kg of _____

A. Rice	B. Flour
C. Oats	D. Sugar

Solution : **(B)** Navneet bought = 4 × 4 = 16 kg of flour.

Example 3 : He bought _____ fewer kilograms of barley than rice.

A. 4	B. 20
C. 8	D. 16

Solution : **(D)** Required weight = weight of rice – weight of barley

$$= 4 \times 6 - 4 \times 2$$
$$= 24 - 8 = 16$$

Example 4 : He bought _____ kg of oats and sugar altogether.

A. 24	B. 16
C. 8	D. 6

Solution : **(A)** Navneet bought = weight of oats + weight of sugar

$$= 4 \times 3 + 4 \times 3$$
$$= 12 + 12 = 24 \text{ kg}$$

Example 5 : Each kilogram of barley cost ₹ 2. He paid ₹ _____ for the barley altogether.

A. 4	B. 16
C. 12	D. 24

Solution : **(B)** Navneet paid = 4 × 2 × 2 = ₹ 16

Example 6 : Navneet spent ₹ 12 on oats. Each kilogram on oats costs ₹ _____.

A. 12	B. 4
C. 3	D. 1

Solution : **(D)** Weight of oats = 4 × 3 = 12 kg

$$\therefore \text{ Required costs } = \frac{12}{12} = 1$$

Multiple Choice Questions

Directions (Q. 1–4) The picture graph below shows the number of cookies 5 children ate. Study the graph and answer the given questions.

Number of cookies each child ate	
A	🍪 🍪 🍪 🍪 🍪
B	🍪 🍪
C	🍪 🍪 🍪
D	🍪 🍪 🍪 🍪
E	🍪 🍪 🍪 🍪 🍪 🍪 🍪

Each 🍪 stands for 3 cookies

1. _____ ate the most number of cookies.
   A. E   B. A
   C. D   D. C

2. "C" ate _____ cookies.
   A. 3   B. 6
   C. 9   D. 12

3. _____ and _____ ate 18 cookies altogether.

   A. A,C   B. B,D
   C. B,C   D. A,B

4. _____ ate 6 cookies more than B.
   A. A   B. C
   C. E   D. None of these

Directions (Q. 5–7) The picture graph below shows favourite pastimes of a group of children. Study the graph and answer the given questions.

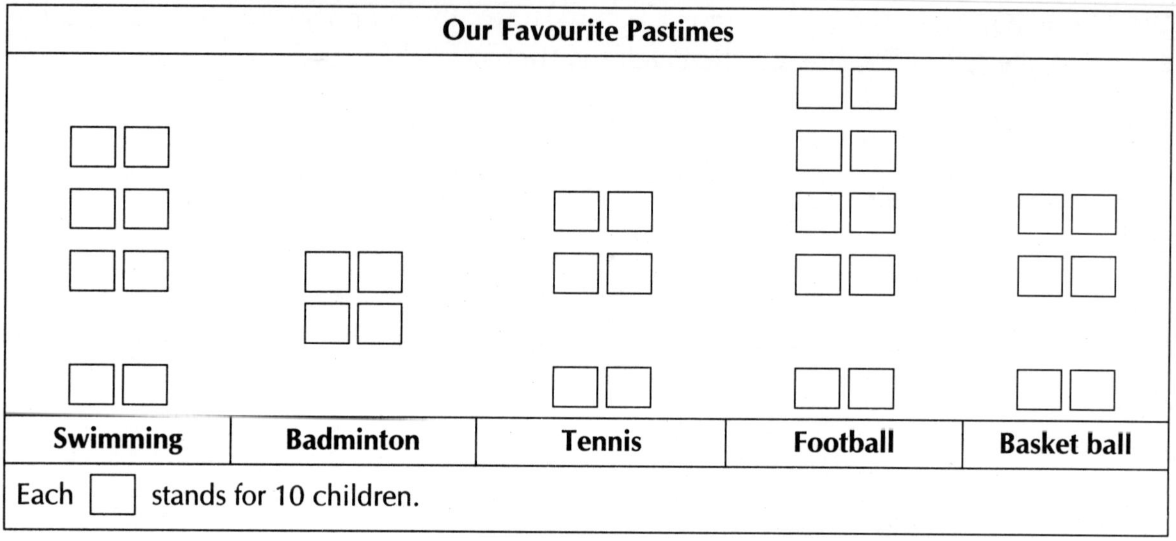

Our Favourite Pastimes				
Swimming	Badminton	Tennis	Football	Basket ball

Each ☐ stands for 10 children.

5. If 45 boys like swimming, _____ girls like swimming.
   A. 45   B. 35   C. 25   D. Can't say

6. _____ is the most popular pastime.
   A. Badminton   B. Tennis   C. Football   D. Basket ball

7. If the same number of boys and girls like basket ball, _____ boys like basket ball.
   A. 100   B. 80   C. 60   D. 30

Directions (Q. 8–9) Use the information below to answer the given questions.

Number of mobile phones sold by Mr. Sharma	
Thursday	
Friday	
Saturday	
Sunday	
Each **stands for 3 mobile phones.**	

8. He sold _____ mobile phones on Saturday and Sunday.

   A. 16   B. 48   C. 75   D. 80

9. If he sold 3 more mobile phones on Friday, he would have sold as many mobile phones as on _____

   A. Thursday   B. Saturday   C. Sunday   D. None of these

Directions (Q. 10–13) The King's Fun Fair is in town! Play the games to win tokens and exchange for toys.

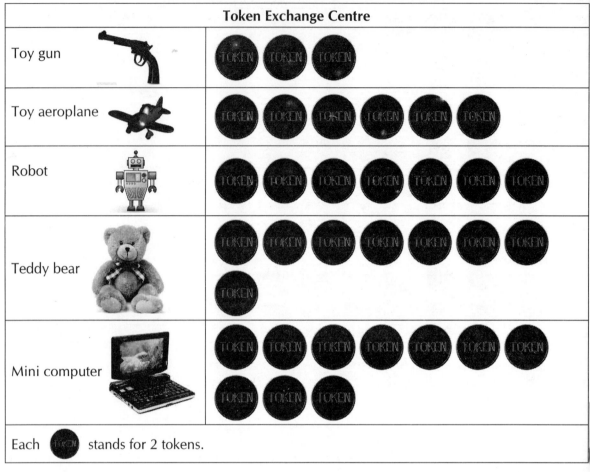

Token Exchange Centre	
Toy gun	TOKEN TOKEN TOKEN
Toy aeroplane	TOKEN TOKEN TOKEN TOKEN TOKEN TOKEN
Robot	TOKEN TOKEN TOKEN TOKEN TOKEN TOKEN TOKEN
Teddy bear	TOKEN TOKEN TOKEN TOKEN TOKEN TOKEN TOKEN TOKEN
Mini computer	TOKEN TOKEN TOKEN TOKEN TOKEN TOKEN TOKEN TOKEN TOKEN TOKEN

Each ⬤ TOKEN stands for 2 tokens.

10. Shraddha won 10 tokens at the fun fair. She needed _____ more tokens to exchange for a toy robot.

   A. 1   B. 2
   C. 3   D. 4

11. Golu won twice as many tokens as Shraddha.
       He could get the _____.
   A. Robot   B. Teddy bear
   C. Toy gun   D. Mini computer

12. Jasmine had just enough tokens to exchange for a teddy bear. If she wanted to exchange her tokens for a 2 toy aeroplanes, she will need _____ more tokens.

   A. 8   B. 6
   C. 4   D. 2

13. Krishna won 30 tokens. He exchanged all of them for two toys. He chose the
    _____ and the _____.
    A. Toy gun, toy plane
    B. Robot, teddy bear
    C. Robot, mini computer
    D. Teddy bear, mini computer

Directions (Q. 14) Look at the picture graph and answer the question.

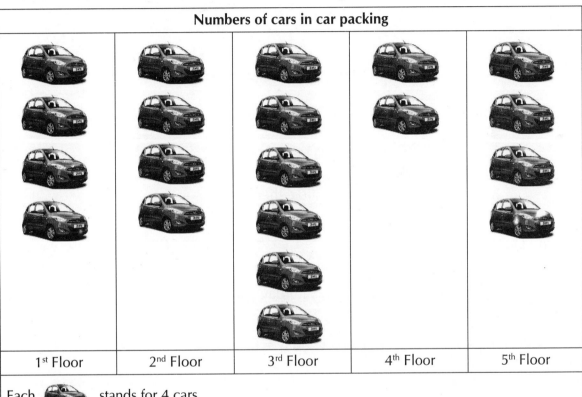

Numbers of cars in car packing				
1st Floor	2nd Floor	3rd Floor	4th Floor	5th Floor

Each stands for 4 cars

14. There were _____ more cars parked on 3rd floor than on the 5th floor.
    A. 4   B. 16   C. 32   D. 12

Answer Key

1. A   2. C   3. B   4. D   5. B   6. C   7. D   8. B   9. C
10. D   11. D   12. A   13. B   14. B

Hints and Solutions

1. Clearly, E ate the most number of cookies.

2. E ate = $3 \times 3 = 9$ cookies

3. B and D ate = $2 \times 3 + 4 \times 3$
   $= 6 + 12 = 18$ cookies altogether.

4. B ate = $2 \times 3 = 6$ cookies
   and D ate = $4 \times 3 = 12$ cookies
   $\therefore$ D ate 6 cookies more than B.

8. Mr. Sharma sold mobile phones on Saturday and Sunday
   $= 3 \times 9 + 3 \times 7 = 27 + 21 = 48$

9. Mr. Sharma sold mobile phones on Friday = $6 \times 3 + 3 = 21$
   Clearly, correct answer is C.

Measurement

9

Learning milestones:
- ☐ Length
- ☐ Mass
- ☐ Volume
- ☐ Money

What is measurement?

Measurement is related to counting or measuring an object. The parameters of measurement are: length, weight, volume, time and money.

For example,

1. Length of an object is measured in meter (m) or centimeter (cm).

   1 meter = 100 cm

2. Mass of an object is measured in kilogram (kg) or gram (gm).

   1 kg = 1000 g.

3. Volume is the amount of liquid, for example, water, juice, milk, in a container. Volume is measured in litre (l) or millilitre (ml).

4. We use a clock or a watch to check the time. Time is measured in hours, minutes and second.

There are 60 minutes (min) in 1 hour (h).

60 seconds (sec) = 1 min

60 min = 1 h

24 hours (h) = 1 day

7 days = 1 week

4 weeks = 1 month

12 months = 1 year

5. Money is measured in Rupee in India.1 rupee = 100 paise

Symbol of Rupee = ₹

For example, how many paise are there in 5 Rupees?

Solution: 100 * 5 = 500

So, there are 500 paise in 5 Rupees.

For Example

1. Look at the figure carefully and answer the following question.

The pencil is _____ cm long.

A. 8   B. 8.5

C. 7.5   D. 7

Ans. C

2. Look at the figure carefully and answer the following question.

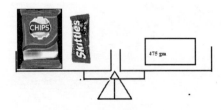

The total mass (weight) of a packet of chips and packet of sweets is 475 gm. The mass of the sweet packet is 250 gm. What is the weight of the chips packet?

A. 200 gm   B. 225 gm

C. 250 gm   D. 325 gm

Hint:- Total weight = 475 gm, weight of the packet of sweets = 250 gm, so weight of the chips packet = 475-220 = 225 gm.

3. Look at the figure carefully and answer the following question.

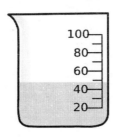

The beaker contains _____ ml of water.

A. 100   B. 40

C. 45   D. 50

4. How many days are there in 5 weeks?

A. 35   B. 36

C. 25   D. 37

Solution: 1 week = 7 days, so 5 weeks = 5 * 7 = 35 days.

5. Sumit earns ₹. 500 per day, so how many rupees will he earn in 30 days?

A. ₹.1500   B. ₹.15000

C. ₹. 10000   D. ₹. 20000

Solution: One day = ₹. 500, so in 30 days = 30 * 500 = ₹. 15000.

Multiple Choice Questions

Direction (1–4) Study the picture and answer the following questions.

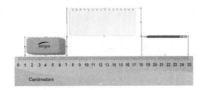

1. The length of the eraser is _____ cm.
   A. 7   B. 6
   C. 6.5   D. 9

2. The length of the pencil is _____ cm.
   A. 6   B. 8
   C. 7   D. 7.5

3. Eraser is _____ cm shorter than the pencil.
   A. 1 cm   B. 3 cm
   C. 2 cm   D. 0.5 cm

4. The length of the notebook is _____ cm.
   A. 18   B. 11
   C. 12   D. 13

5. Look at the figure carefully and answer the following question.

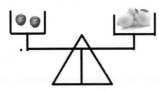

If the weight of three apples is 250 grams, and all the three lemons are of same weight, then what is the weight of one lemon?
   A. 75.55   B. 73.33
   C. 83.33   D. 85.33

6. Look at the figure carefully and answer the following question.

Which is the heaviest?
   A. Grapes   B. Pineapple
   C. Apple   D. Banana

Direction (7–8) Look at pictures carefully and answer the following questions.

7. If one ⬤ is equals to 1000 grams, what would be the weight of bricks?
   A. 2000 gm   B. 10000 gm
   C. 8000 gm   D. 25000 gm

8. If one ⬤ is equals to 1000 grams, what would be the total weight of water melon and bricks?
   A. 4000 gm   B. 2000 gm
   C. 8000 gm   D. 16000 gms

Direction (9–10) Look at pictures carefully and answer the following questions.

National Science Olympiad – Class 2

9. The tree is _____ m tall.
   A. 25　　　　　　B. 50
   C. 55　　　　　　D. 23.6

10. The boy is _____ m tall.
    A. 23.6　　　　　B. 55 m
    C. 1.4 m　　　　D. 1.5 m

Direction (11–13) Look at pictures carefully and answer the following questions.

11. If three glasses is equals to 500 ml, then the jug can hold _____ ml of water.
    A. 950　　　　　　B. 850
    C. 750　　　　　　D. 1000

12. If one table spoon is equals to 15 ml, then 1 glass is equal to _____.
    A. 250　　　　　　B. 150
    C. 100　　　　　　D. 125

13. A jug is filled with eight glasses and one glass is filled with 10 table spoons, then how many spoons can fill a jug?
    A. 80　　　　　　B. 70
    C. 100　　　　　D. 180

14. If 750 ml of milk is required to prepare 500 gm of curd, then how much milk is required to prepare 2000 gm of curd?
    A. 3500　　　　　B. 2000
    C. 2500　　　　　D. 3000

    A vase of water can fill up 6 cups. A bucket of water can fill up 12 cups. A tub of water can fill 24 cups.

Based on the above information, answer the following questions.

15. Somya needs _____ vases to fill up two buckets.
    A. 2　　　　　　　B. 3
    C. 5　　　　　　　D. 4

16. Somya needs _____ vase(s) and _____ buckets(s) to fill up a tub of water.
    A. 2, 4　　　　　　B. 3, 4
    C. 4, 2　　　　　　D. 4, 1

17. Somya goes for music classes at 3.30 pm every day. The time being shown by the wall clock now is

How much time is left for her class now?
    A. 60 minutes　　B. 90 minutes
    C. 100 minutes　D. 110 minutes

18. Which clock shows half past 10?

A. 　　B.

C.　　D.

19. How much time does hour hand of a clock take to complete three rounds?
    A. 60 minutes　　B. 1 hour
    C. 180 minutes　D. 2 hours

20. How many minutes are there in one day?

    A. 1440   B. 550

    C. 1660   D. 1760

21. Sanjay takes 10 minutes to complete writing one page. How much time does he take to complete writing 6 pages?

    A. 600   B. 60

    C. 65   D. 76

Direction (22–24): Study the given table below carefully and answer the following questions.

Item	Price
	₹. 75
	₹. 175
	₹. 100
	₹. 100
	₹. 45

22. Shruti wants to buy 1 notebook, 2 geometry boxes and 2 sets of colour pencils. She needs _____ altogether.

    A. ₹. 200   B. ₹. 90

    C. ₹. 290   D. ₹. 245

23. Anaya wants to buy 1 water bottle, 1 lunch box and 1 notebook. She has Rs 200. so How much more money she needs to buy all these items?

    A. ₹. 100   B. ₹. 175

    C. ₹. 75   D. ₹. 200

24. Vinay brought a textbook and he gave the cashier Rs. 100. He receives ₹._____ change.

    A. ₹. 20   B. ₹. 25

    C. ₹. 50   D. ₹. 55

25. Look at the given fruit box. It has 16 fruits. Each fruit cost Rs. 3. How much does 5 fruit boxes cost?

    A. ₹. 240   B. ₹. 440

    C. ₹. 550   D. ₹. 300

Answer Key

1. B   2. C   3. A   4. B   5. C   6. B   7. C   8. D   9. A
10. C   11. D   12. B   13. A   14. D   15. D   16. C   17. D   18. C
19. C   20. A   21 B   22 C   23 C   24 B   25 A

Hints *and* Solutions

1. Eraser starting from 1 and ending at 7 cm, so length of the eraser is
   = 7 cm – 1 cm = 6 cm.

5. 2 Apples = 3 lemons. Weight of 2 apples = 250 grams, so weight of 3 lemons = 250 gm.
   So, weight of 1 lemon = 250/3 = 83.33 gm.

7. One water melon = 1000 gm, so 8 water melons = 1000 * 8 = 8000. So, as per the above picture 8 water melons = bricks.
   So, total weight of bricks = 8000 gm.

9. Length of tower = 80 m, distance between tower and tree is = 55 m, so the length of the tree = 80 – 55 = 25 m.

10. Length of tree = 25 m, distance between tree and the boy = 23.6 m, so the length of the boy = 25 - 23.6 = 1.4 m.

18. Half past 10 means 10.30.

19. One round = 60 minutes, so 3 rounds = 60 * 3 = 180

20. Number of minutes in one day = 24 * 60 = 1440.

Geometrical Shapes

10

Shape is defined as an external boundary or an outline of an object. An outline that provides the geometric information is called the geometric shape of an object.

There are several kinds of shapes around us. We can observe them in our daily life also. Some of them are described below.

Geometrical Lines

1. Vertical line

A line that moves from up to down, on a page is called the vertical line.

2. Horizontal line

A line that moves from left to right across the page is called a horizontal line.

3. Slanting line

A line that is straight but leans (/) towards another direction is known as a slanting line.

4. Curved line

A line which is not straight and has no sharp edges is called a curve line or a curve.

Examples

1. Which two types of geometrical lines form the figure shown below?

   A. Four vertical line
   B. Two vertical and two horizontal line
   C. One vertical and one slanting line
   D. Four slanting lines

Solution:

There are two vertical and two horizontal lines in the given figure.

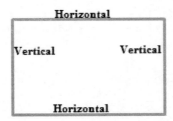

2. Count the curved lines in the given figure.

   A. Six   B. Two
   C. Five   D. Four

Solution

There are five curved lines in the given figure.

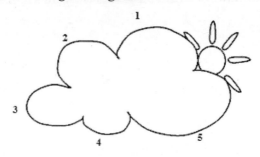

Plane Geometrical Shapes

1. Triangle

Triangle is a shape, which has three sides or edges. Triangle may vary according to the sizes of the sides, for example: A triangle with three equal sides, a triangle with unequal sides.

2. Square

A shape that has four equally-sized sides is called a square. It looks like a box.

3. Rectangle

Rectangle also looks like a box. It has four sides, with two sets of equal sides, which are opposite to each other.

4. Circle

It is a round figure with no corners.

Solid Geometrical Shapes

1. Cone

A cone has two faces, one is curved and another is plane. It has one corner. Cone shape is similar to the triangle but it has a circle as a base.

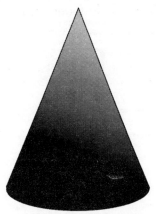

2. Cylinder

A cylinder has three faces, one curved surface along with two plane surfaces. It has no corners.

3. Cube

A shape with six square faces, 12 edges and 8 corners is called a cube. It resembles a carton.

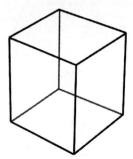

4. Cuboid

Cuboid is a shape with six-plane-rectangle faces and eight corners. It has 12 edges.

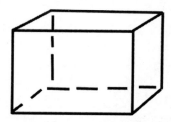

5. Sphere

Sphere has only one face with no edges or corners.

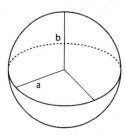

Examples

1. Count the number of triangles in the given figure.

A. 7   B. 6
C. 8   D. 5

Solution

There are seven triangles in the given figure.

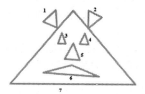

2. The following figure is made up of _____ number of squares and _____ number of rectangles.

    A. 2, 5   B. 5, 2

    C. 4, 2   D. 2, 4

Solution

The figure is made up of five squares and two rectangles.

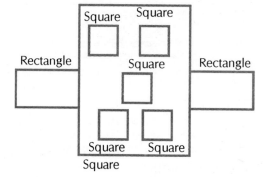

Multiple Choice Questions

1. The figure given below is made up of _____ triangles.

   A. 5
   B. 6
   C. 7
   D. 8

2. Which two shapes form the given figure?

   A. rhombus and square
   B. triangle and square
   C. kite and rhombus
   D. rectangle and triangle

3. Which two types of geometrical shapes are hidden in the given picture?

   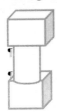

   A. Square and cylinder
   B. Rectangle and cylinder
   C. Cubes and cylinder
   D. Rectangle and cubes

4. How many lines are not straight lines in the given figure?

   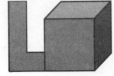

   A. 11
   B. 10
   C. 9
   D. 3

5. How many circles are there in the given face?

   A. 1
   B. 2
   C. 3
   D. 4

6. How many triangles are there in the given figure?

   A. 6
   B. 3
   C. 2
   D. 5

7. There are _____ number of _____ in the given figure.

   A. 6, squares
   B. 6, rectangles
   C. 4, squares
   D. 4, rectangles

8. Which of the following shape(s) cannot be found in the given figure?

   A. Circle
   B. Triangle
   C. Square
   D. Rectangle

9. How many standing lines are there in the given figure?

A. 4
B. 3
C. 6
D. 5

10. Which two shapes do not meet?

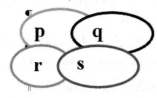

A. p and q
B. q and r
C. p and s
D. p and r

11. How many circles are there in the given figure?

A. 10
B. 21
C. 22
D. 20

12. Which of the following shapes has the largest number of sides?

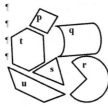

A. p
B. q
C. t
D. s

13. There are _____ more squares than the triangles in the given figure.

A. 4
B. 6
C. 5
D. 2

14. How many slanting lines are there in the given figure?

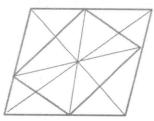

A. 10
B. 9
C. 8
D. 12

15. The following figure is made up of _____ number of circles.

A. 15
B. 8
C. 10
D. 9

16. Count the number of straight lines, curved lines and circles.

	Straight line	Curved Line	Circle
A.	2	3	3
B.	3	3	3
C.	3	3	1
D.	3	3	2

17. The given figure is made up of _____ number of curved lines.

A. 4   B. 3
C. 2   D. 1

18. How many squares are there in the given figure?

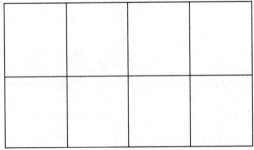

A. 4   B. 11
C. 8   D. 6

19. Identify the shapes in the figure given below.

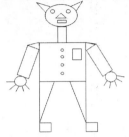

A. Circle, rectangle, triangle, square and Lines
B. Circle, triangle, and square
C. Circle, rectangle, and triangle
D. Circle and rectangle

20. How many triangles are there in the given figure?

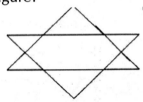

A. 6   B. 5
C. 8   D. 9

Answer Key

1. C   2. A   3. C   4. D   5. C   6. B   7. A   8. C   9. A
10. B   11. D   12. C   13. A   14. A   15. C   16. B   17. A   18. C
19. A   20. C

Section 3
Achievers Section

High Order Thinking Skills (HOTS)

1. **Select the correct options from column I and column II.**

   I. A black bear eats different things, such as grasses, roots, and berries. It also eats insects, fish, and other small animals. Which of these BEST describes a black bear?

   II. A wolf eats deer, bison, moose, etc. Which of these BEST describes a wolf?

	I	II
A.	Omnivore	Carnivore
B.	Herbivore	Carnivore
C.	Omnivore	Omnivore
D.	Producer	Carnivore

2. **Study the given flow chart. Identify one example of the following and select the correct option.**

   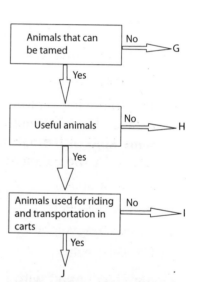

   i. Animal 'G' eats the flesh of dead animals and animal 'I' gives honey.

   ii. Animal 'H' is a scavenger and animal 'J' is used for riding.

	G	H	I	J
A.	Jackal	Hen	Sheep	Goat
B.	Crocodile	Hyenas	Honeybee	Horse
C.	Vulture	Sheep	Snake	Camel
D.	Hyena	Horse	Giraffe	Chicken

3. **The photograph below shows a cactus plant covered with sharp spines.**

   What are the spines for?

   A. They lose almost no water at all
   B. They provide support to the plant
   C. They attract bees
   D. They carry food to the flower

4. **Identify one example of the following and select the correct option.**

   i.   Plant 'G' lives for many years and plant 'I' has a weak stem.
   ii. Plant 'H' grows in water and plant 'J' grows on mountains and hills.

	G	H	I	J
A.	Peepal	Grape	Money plant	Oak
B.	Ashoka	Ferns	Cactus	Cedar
C.	Neem	Lotus	Money plant	Oak
D.	Mango	Grape	Ferns	Ashoka

5. **Which thing near this house will wash away the MOST during heavy rain?**

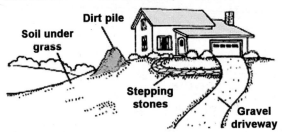

   A. Gravel driveway
   C. Stepping stones
   B. Dirt pile
   D. Soil under grass

6. **The following picture shows a balance. One side of the balance holds an empty balloon. The other side holds the same kind of balloon full of air. Which property of air is shown by the balance?**

   A. Air is solid
   B. Air has heat
   C. Air has weight
   D. Air is energy

7. **Match column I with column II and select the correct option.**

	I		II
a.	Children's Day	1.	Mahatma Gandhi
b.	Teacher's Day	2.	Lal Bahadur Shastri
c.	Raj Ghat, New Delhi	3.	Chacha Nehru
d.	2nd October	4.	Dr Sarvepalli Radhakhrishnan

   A. a-4; b-3; c-1; d-2
   B. a-3; b-4; c-1; d-2
   C. a-4; b-2; c-1; d-3
   D. a-1; b-3; c-4; d-2

8. The diagram below shows the digestive system of the human body.
   The part marked _____ removes water from the undigested food.

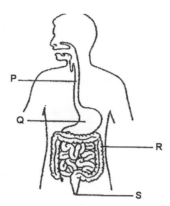

A. P   B. S
C. R   D. Q

9. Refer the given diagram of the solar system.
   I.   Which of them denotes the correct position of the moon?
   II. Who was the first person to step on the moon?

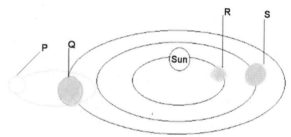

	I	II
A.	Q	Neil Armstrong
B.	P	Neil Armstrong
C.	R	Alyssa Carson
D.	S	Kalpana Chawla

10. Match column I with column II and select the correct option.

	I	II
a.	Kutcha house	1. Made on wheels
b.	Pucca house	2. Made of bamboo, mud, straw, leaves, etc.
c.	Igloo	3. Made of wood, bricks, cement, steel, etc.
d.	Caravan	4. Made of snow

A. a-2; b-4; c-1; d-3
B. a-2; b-1; c-4; d-3
C. a-2; b-3; c-4; d-1
D. a-1; b-2; c-3; d-4

11. **Different kinds of food help us in different ways. Some foods give us energy. Some foods help us grow and some foods keep us healthy.**

I. The food items shown in the given pictures fall under which food group?

II. Which of them is not an animal food product?

	I	II
A.	Protective foods	Eggs
B.	Body building food	Pulse
C.	Roughage-giving food	Milk
D.	Energy-giving food	Pulse

12. **The region of the earth near the _____ receives almost the same amount of sunlight throughout the year. This region always remains hot and has days and night of equal duration. On the other hand the _____ receive(s) sunlight only for six months and remain(s) dark for the next six months.**

   Select the correct sequence of words to fill the blanks in the given passage.

   A. Southern hemisphere; Northern hemisphere

   B. Equator; poles

   D. Axis; equator

   D. Northern hemisphere; Southern hemisphere

13. **Match column I with column II and select the correct option.**

	I		II
a.	Police man	1.	Fire station
b.	Doctor	2.	Police station
c.	Postman	3.	Hospital
d.	Fireman	4.	Post office

   A. a-2; b-3; c-4; d-1   B. a-1; b-3; c-4; d-2

   C. a-2; b-1; c-4; d-3   D. a-2; b-3; c-1; d-4

14. When a cup of water at room temperature is put in a freezer, the water's state of matter will change from:

    A Liquid to gas   B. Gas to liquid

    C. Liquid to solid   D. Solid to liquid

15. The given diagram shows the weather conditions. Which season has the 'X' weather condition?

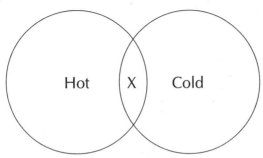

    A. Monsoon   B. Spring

    C. Summer   D. Winter

16. Read the conversation given below and select the correct option.

Somya: I keep my things in their proper place after playing.

Babita: If you do not, you or someone else might trip on them.

    A. Babita is right, while Somya is wrong

    B. Both Babita and Somya are right

    C. Babita explained the hazards hidden in an untidy room

    D. Both B and C

17. The following picture shows that the water cycle process occurs in the direction of arrows starting from point 4.

A. Condensation; evaporation; precipitation

B. Evaporation; condensation; precipitation

C. Evaporation; precipitation; condensation

D. Precipitation;condensation; evaporation

18. **Match column I with column II and select the correct option.**

	I		II
a.	Ship of the desert		1. Elephant
b.	Ship of Himalayan region		2. Reindeer
c.	Animal as transport in South-east Asia		3. Camel
d.	Animal as transport in Arctic and sub-Arctic Nordic		4. Yak

A. a-3; b-4; c-1; d-2   B. a-3; b-2; c-1; d-4

C. a-1; b-2; c-4; d-3   D. a-1; b-3; c-4; d-2

19. **Find the odd one out.**

A. E-mail; Twitter; Facebook; You tube

B. Twitter; Facebook; LinkedIn; You tube

C. Facebook; LinkedIn; You tube;Twitter

D. LinkedIn; Facebook; Twitter; You tube

20. **Match column I with column II and select the correct option.**

	I	II
a.	Metro train	1. Runs on diesel
b.	Bicycle	2. Runs on electricity
c.	Truck	3. Runs by animal
d.	Bullock cart	4. Runs by manpower

A. a-3; b-2;c-4; d-1   B. a-2; b-4;c-3; d-1

C. a-4; b-2;c-1; d-3   D. a-2; b-4;c-1; d-3

Answer Key

1. A   2. B   3. A   4. C   5. B   6. C   7. B   8. C   9. B
10. C   11. B   12. B   13. A   14. C   15. B   16. D   17. B   18. A
19. A   20. D

Section 4
Subjective Section

Short Answer Questions

1. **What happens if we keep a plant in an artificially-lit room without sunlight?**

   Answer: For good growth of a plant, it needs sufficient sunlight. Artificial light lacks the properties of sunlight. Due to this, plants kept in artificially-lit rooms turn yellow and their leaves start drooping. Flowering plants also stop flowering when kept in artificial lighting.

2. **What would happen to the plants if some of these habitats in the following were changed?**

A. **Water in a pond is reduced**

   Answer: The plants and animals which are present in the pond will start dying.

B. **Desert starts getting excessive rain**

   Answer: Desert plants are adapted to dry conditions, but if these plants start getting more water, these plants will start turning yellow in colour, get more and more mushy and turn dark reddish-brown, like a rotten apple.

3. **Why do people destroy habitats?**

   Answer: People destroy habitats to fulfill their own needs like making residential spaces, factories, and offices. More and more construction work in suburban areas disturb the ecological balance of the planet.

4. **What is the difference between honey and sugar?**

   Answer: Honey and sugar are sweetening agents but the source of obtaining them is different. Honey is obtained from honey bees whereas sugar is obtained from sugarcane, which is a plant.

5. **Why do aquatic plants have broad leaves with a waxy coating?**

   Answer: Aquatic plants have broad leaves with a waxy coating so that they can float on the surface of water. The waxy coating prevents them from sinking in water.

HOTS

1. What can be the most prominent difference between leaf of a pine tree and leaf of a mango tree?
2. Why do cactus plants have spines?

---

6. **What is the difference between a panda, a polar bear, and a black bear?**

   Answer: The difference between these three is that they live in different habitats and have different food habits. Pandas are plant eaters, polar bears are almost entirely carnivores, whereas black bears are omnivores.

7. **What will happen if all animals become herbivores?**

   Answer: If all animals turn into herbivores then they will need lot of grass and plants to eat and this will disturb the balance in nature.

8. **From the options given below who would die of hunger if only seeds are fed to them?**

   Answer: A cat would die of hunger as cat's teeth are not structured to eat seeds.

9. **How will you define the habitat of a bird? Is it land? Is it tree or land? Is it air, tree, or land? Describe.**

   Answer: Birds are generally known as aerial animals, but they live in various places. Some live on trees, some on land, and some in water and land. So we cannot strictly categorize them as aerial animals.

10. **How do different animals communicate?**

    Answer: Animals make different kinds of sounds to communicate. Some are mentioned below:

Animals	Sound
lions	roar
mice	squeak
horses	whinny
ducks	quack
dogs	bark
deer	grunt
crows	caw
cows	moo
cats	meow
birds	chirp
bears	growl
goats, giraffe, sheep	bleat
pigs	snort
sparrows	chirp
squirrels	squeak

11. What are internal organs?

Answer: Internal organs are those parts of our body which are inside our body and cannot be seen from the outside. Examples: Brain, heart, lungs, stomach, and kidneys.

12. How do our bones and muscles work together to make our body work like a machine?

Answer: Muscles work together with bones to help you move. Lots of muscles are attached to your bones, and when you tighten your muscle, your bone moves, too.

13. What is the skeletal and muscular system and how do they make the body work?

Answer: Under our skin, we have bones that form skeleton. The skeleton gives our body shape and structure. Without a skeleton we would look like a puddle of bumpy skin on the floor. Bones are articulated and can move with the help of muscles. Muscles are connected to our bones and stretch like a rubber band to pull on the bones and make them move. We can wiggle our fingers and toes and sit and stand because of muscles and bones. The skeleton also protects us. Our skull protects our soft brain just like a helmet. Our ribs protect our vital organs. Joints are where bones come together and bend. Knuckles, knees, and elbows are examples of joints.

14. What can we do to keep our bones and muscles healthy?

Answer: Exercise involves moving and putting pressure on the muscles and bones. Walking and running are forms of exercise. Exercise builds strong muscles and bones. Eating good and healthy food also helps make our bones and muscles strong. Dairy products like milk, cheese, and ice cream are good for bones. The sugars in fruits and vegetables give us energy for our bones and muscles. Eating protein helps build muscle. Protein is found in meats, eggs, and beans.

5. Why is food important?

Answer: Food is essential for our body to:

♦ develop, replace, and repair cells and tissues;

- produce energy to keep warm, move, and work;
- carry out chemical processes such as the digestion of food;
- protect against, resist, and fight infection and recover from sickness

16. What do you mean by "eating well"?

Answer: Eating well means eating a variety of foods. No single food contains all the nutrients that our bodies need, except for breast milk for babies up to the age of six months. Eating a variety of foods will supply the nutrients that are essential for our bodies. By taking care to choose foods that are in season and locally available, eating can be enjoyable, healthy, and affordable.

17. Why should we drink plenty of water?

Answer: Our body is composed of about 60 per cent water. The functions of water include digestion, absorption, circulation, creation of saliva, transportation of nutrients, and maintenance of body temperature and so it is essential to drink plenty of water every day.

18. Why is brushing teeth important?

Answer: After eating food, some food particles may remain stuck to your teeth. These food particles form a medium for the germs to grow, harm your gums and teeth, and cause bad breath. Brushing of teeth every day does not let the germs grow. Brushing of teeth before going to bed is a very good habit.

19. What is first-aid?

Answer: First-aid is the immediate medical help given to an injured and sick person before the doctor arrives. The main aim of giving first-aid is to: 1. save lives 2. keep the victim comfortable till medical help arrives.

Common emergencies that need first-aid are: bleeding wounds, poisoning, insect bites, burns, etc.

HOTS

7. What is the difference between the proteins found in egg and those found in pulses? Explain in one line.

8. What will happen to a child's growth if he/she does not have milk and milk products at all?

---

20. Why do we not find houseboats in Rajasthan?

Answer: Houseboats are designed in such a way that they float on water. They are also called Float houses. Rajasthan is a desert and water is not easily available there. It is also known as the dry region of India. This is why we would not find houseboats in Rajasthan.

21. **Roofs are a very important part of a house. Why?**

    Answer: The main purpose of a roof is to protect the house in all types of weather with minimum maintenance. A roof must be strong enough to withstand snow and wind loads.

22. **Sloping roofs are good for places which have snowfall. True or false?**

    Answer: Yes, it is true. Because slanting roofs facilitate snow removal much better than flat roofs.

23. **What type of clothes we should take with us when we are going on a holiday to Assam in December? And why?**

    Answer: The climate in Assam is cold and there is rainfall in those months. So, if we are going on a holiday to Assam in December, we should take woollen clothes and well as raincoats and umbrellas with us.

24. **We wear different clothes in different seasons. Why?**

    Answer: We wear different clothes in different seasons according to the suitability of the cloth. It's all about adaption of the climatic conditions. For example, in summer it is suitable to wear cotton clothes as they absorb sweat. And in winter it is suitable to wear woollen clothes as they do not let the heat get out (i.e., they retain heat) and protect the body from the chill and cold.

HOTS

9. What are roof-top gardens?

10. It rains and snows in the mountains. What would happen if the houses there had flat roofs?

---

25. **In a class, the teacher gave the activity of making a family tree to the students. Few students took a long time to make the tree and few made it quickly. Can you guess why some students took longer to make the family tree?**

    Answer: Children who have small and nuclear families will take less time to make family tree while those who have big and joint families will take long time to complete the activity as they have more family members.

26. **There are two friends, Rita and Maria. Maria meets her grandparents every summer during her vacation whereas Rita sees her grandparents daily. What is the difference between their families?**

    Answer: Rita lives in a joint family so she meets her grandparents daily, while Maria lives in a nuclear family so she meets her grandparents only during her vacations.

27. **India is called the "land of festivals". Why?**

    Answer: India is called land of festivals because in India, people from various religions live together in harmony and every religion has its own festivals. Indians celebrate all these festivals together.

28. Why are National Festivals called so?

Answer: Some festivals are celebrated by the whole nation. These are called National Festivals.

29. What is the difference between grocer and green grocer?

Answer: A grocer (shopkeeper) sells goods like sugar, grains, pulses, salt, and many other things, while a green grocer only sells vegetables and fruits.

HOTS

11. Can we resemble our classmates, too? How?

12. Discuss which occupation you would like to take up as a career in the future. Give reasons.

---

30. Why should I wear a cycle helmet when riding my bike?

Answer: A cycle helmet will protect us if we fall off, or are knocked off, our bike. If we don't wear a cycle helmet and we crash, we will be badly hurt.

31. What is a zebra crossing?

Answer: A zebra crossing is a crossing where black and white stripes are painted onto the road. These crossings give pedestrians the right of way. We must make sure that all traffic has stopped before we use the crossing.

32. Why is it important to stay away from substations?

Answer: If there is a substation in your neighbourhood, it is important to steer clear. There is a lot of high-voltage electricity inside – and you should not touch anything inside or you will get hurt.

33. With which term is Wi-Fi related?

Answer: Wi-Fi is an acronym for "wireless fidelity" and it refers to a wireless network for computers.

34. Who invented the telephone?

Answer: In the 1870s, two inventors Elisha Gray and Alexander Graham Bell independently designed devices called 'the telephone'.

HOTS

13. How does transportation affect the availability of goods?

14. Name one mode of communication which is private as well as public. Justify your answer.

---

35. **Wet clothes take a long time to dry in the rainy season. Why?**

   Answer: Wet clothes take more time to dry in the rainy season because in the rainy season, there is already a lot of water vapour in the atmosphere and the rate of evaporation becomes low. The Sun's rays are also hidden by the clouds, due to which the drying is slow.

36. **What will happen if a burning candle is covered with a glass jar?**

   Answer: If a burning candle is covered with a glass jar, it will continue to burn for some time, and after some time it will go out. This is because it uses all the air (oxygen) inside the glass jar. Once the oxygen is all used up, the candle goes out. This proves that oxygen is necessary to burn fire.

37. **We should breathe clean air. Why?**

   Answer: We should breathe clean air because if we breathe dirty air, we will fall sick because of the germs present in it.

38. **What are "canals" and what the purpose behind building them?**

   Answer: Canal is an artificial waterway for irrigation. They are made to supply water from rivers and reservoir to far-off places and to the fields.

39. **Into which water bodies does the water collect when it rains?**

   Answer: When it rains, some of the water goes into soil. It collects deep under the ground. People dig wells and tubewells to bring this water out. Some of the rain water also collects in ponds, rivers, and lakes.

HOTS

15. Why should we stay indoors when a strong wind blows?
16. Why do we often see water droplets on leaves and other objects outside our house in the winter season?

---

40. **Why are plains good for growing crops?**

   Answer: Plains often have rich soil. For this reason, many plains are used for growing crops or grazing animals.

41. **How are plateaus formed?**

   Answer: Plateaus can form when forces within the Earth uplift rock layers. They can also form when sections of the Earth's crust are forced into each other. Some plateaus are caused by volcanic activity. Layers of lava build up over time to form plateaus.

42. **Earth is not the only planet with clouds. Name the other planets that also have clouds.**

   Answer: Other planets like Venus, Mars, Jupiter, Neptune, Uranus, and Saturn have clouds too.

43. **How is the "Phases of Moon" cycle caused?**

   Answer: This cycle is caused by the Sun's light and the Moon's orbit. Those parts of the Moon that receive the Sun's light glow with reflected light. This makes the Moon appear bright white. The part of the Moon that is under the shadow of the Earth, looks black or dark, much like the night sky. Depending on where the Moon is in its orbit, we see either its lighted side or dark side, or some mix or combination of both the sides.

44. **Can we see a rainbow at night? If yes, give reasons.**

   Answer: No, we cannot see a rainbow at night because rainbows appear in the sky when there is bright sunlight and rain. Sunlight is known as visible or white light and is actually a mixture of colours.

HOTS

17. Why do people carry umbrellas with them when the Sun shines?
18. What will happen if the Earth stops rotating?

Section 5
Model Papers

Model Test Paper – 1

1. **Which of the following animal does not lay eggs?**

   A.    B.

   C.    D.

2. **Bees and butterflies collect _____ from flowers.**
   A. Colour   B. Oil
   C. Nectar   D. All of these

3. **Look at the given flow chart. Study it carefully.**

   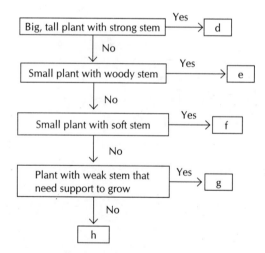

   Which of the following statements is correct?
   A. h represents coconut tree
   B. g is a creeper
   C. e is a shrub
   D. d represents coriander plant

4. Which of the following are parts of a seed?

A.

B.

C.

D. B and C both

5. Which organ(s) help us breathe?

A.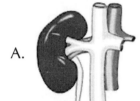

B.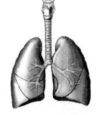

C.

D.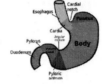

6. Which of the following is not related to sense organ?

A. Sight   B. Smell

C. Digestion   D. Sound

7. This fruit is used in making Indian beverages:

A.

B.

C.

D. All of the above

8. Study the given flow chart and select the correct option which can fill the empty spaces "d", "e", and "f".

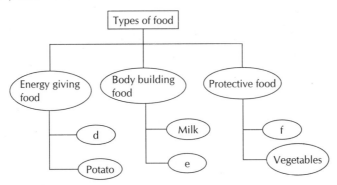

A. d-jaggery, e-butter, f-nuts

B. d-egg, e-fish, f-soyabean

C. d-rice, e-egg, f-nut

D. d-bread, e-fruits, f-cheese

9. In which of these places do people make light houses of wood and paper?

A. London   B. Mumbai

C. Kashmir   D. Japan

10. Which of the following can be run by gas engines?

1.    2.

3.    4.

A. 1 and 2   B. 1 and 4

C. 3 and 4   D. All of the above

11. Dussehra is celebrated on the _____ day of Navaratra.

A. 5th   B. 10th

C. 14th   D. 2nd

12. _____'s birthday is celebrated on 5th September.

A. Dr. Radhakrishnan   B. Dr. Rajendra Prasad

C. Bal Gangadhar Tilak   D. Lala Lajpat Rai

13. Match the following

   a. Green-grocer   i.   Baked bread
   b. Chemist   ii. Flies an aeroplane
   c. Baker   iii. Sell medicine
   d. Magician   iv. Sells vegetables
   e. Pilot   v.   Shows magic

   A. a-iv, b-iii, c-i, d-v, e-ii
   B. a-iv, b-iii, c-i, d-ii, e-v
   C. a-iv, b-i, c-iii, d-v, e-ii
   D. a-iii, b-iv, c-i, d-v, e-ii

14. Ananya's school name is Ananya Juyal but at home everyone calls her Gauri. This other name is called:

   A. Surname   B. First name
   C. Nick name   D. Pet name

15. This person shown in the following picture is:

   A. A person driving the car
   B. A person making furniture
   C. A person painting the car
   D. A person painting the house

16. A person sells the items shown in the following image. Name the person.

 A. Florist   B. Stationer

 C. Grocer   D. Chemist

17. Which of these are incorrect statements regarding safety rules?

 1. Avoid swimming with grown-up near you

 2. Do not play rough games in the pool

 3. Always take a rubber tube with you

 4. Always swim in the deep end

 A. 1 and 2   B. 1 and 4

 C. 1, 2, and 4   D. All of them

18. Which of these is not a good habit?

 A. Do not throw garbage on road

 B. Throw waste into the dustbin

 C. Always take excess food than needed

 D. Keep food covered

19. A _____ is a group of stars that forms an image.

 A. Solar system   B. Constellation

 C. Planet   D. The Sun

20. At which the Moon be during an eclipse of the Sun?

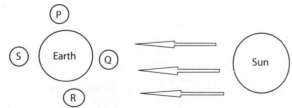

 A. R   B. Q

 C. P   D. S

21. Which common thing, the following objects need?

A. Thread

B. Sun

C. Water

D. Air

22. Which statement is true?

A. Air has no weight

B. Air stays in one place

C. Air takes up space

D. Air is blue in colour

23. Identify the following instrument:

A. Wind vane   B. Lactometer

C. Balance   D. Rain gauge

24. In how many states can water exist?

    A. 1   B. 2

    C. 3   D. 4

25. Which fibre is used to make a sweater?

A.    B.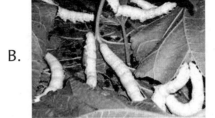

C.    D.

Answer Key

1. B   2. C   3. C   4. D   5. B   6. C   7. D   8. C   9. D

10. A   11. B   12. A   13. A   14. C   15. B   16. C   17. B   18. C

19. B   20. B   21. D   22. C   23. A   24. C   25. C

Achievers Section

1. Study the table below carefully.

Characteristics	Plants			
	P	**Q**	**R**	**S**
Does the plant live in water?	No	Yes	Yes	No
Are its fruits poisonous?	Yes	No	No	No
Does its fruits grow singly?	No	Yes	No	Yes

Based on the information in the above table, which one of the following statements is most likely to be true?

A. Plant S grows on land and its fruits are poisonous and grow in a bunch

B. Plant Q grows in water and it has poisonous fruit that grow singly

C. Plant R grows in water and it has non-poisonous fruits that grow singly

D. Plant P grows on land and it has poisonous fruits that grow in a bunch

2. Read the given passage and answer the questions that follow.

> Many wild animals are being killed by humans for sport, food, or medicines. As a result, some animals have become very few in numbers. Such animals are called endangered animals.

I. Select an example of endangered animals.

II. Where are endangered animals kept for their protection?

	I	II
A.	Sheep	Zoo
B.	Cow	National park
C.	Rabbit	Park
D.	Rhinoceros	National parks

3. Study the given flowchart and select the correct option.

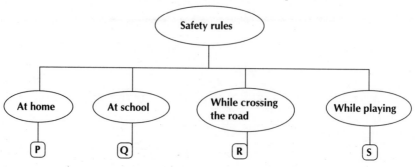

A. Q-Do not stand in the queue

B. P-Do not touch stoves, heaters, toasters

C. S-Do not fly kites in open fields

D. R-Do not cross the road when the traffic light is red

4. Study the given family tree and select the correct option.

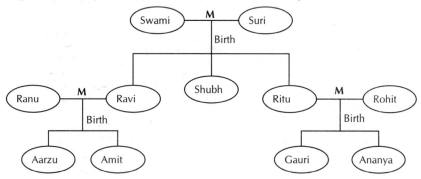

M stands for married

A. Ravi and Ritu are husband and wife

B. Ananya and Amit are cousins

C. Suri is Ritu's aunt

D. Amit is Swami's son-in-law

5. In which of the following arrangements, will the moon cast a shadow on the earth?

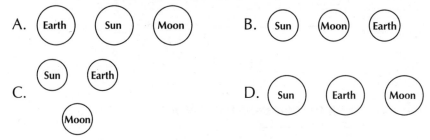

Answer Key

1. D   2. D   3. B   4. B   5. B

Model Test Paper – 2

1. **Look at the following food chains. Write the correct word in the box.**

Leaf, tadpole, human

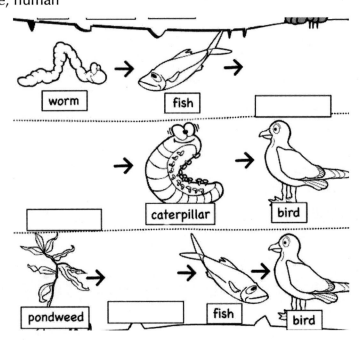

A. Human, leaf, tadpole
B. Tadpole, human, leaf
C. Leaf, human, tadpole
D. Leaf, tadpole, human

2. **Classify the animals according to their external features:**

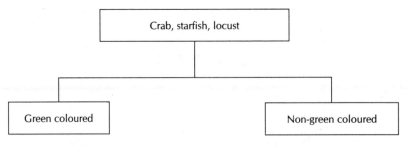

A. Locust; crab, starfish
B. Starfish; locust, crab
C. Crab; starfish, locust
D. Both A and B

3. Which of the following is not a plant?

A.

B.

C.

D.

4. This medicine is prepared by the trunk (bark) of a plant and used to cure malaria:
   A. Cold syrup   B. Quinine
   C. Cough syrup   D. Penicillin

5. Look at the picture given below:
   Can you list the parts of the body that help the deer escape from the lion?

   A. Ears, legs, heart   B. Legs, eyes, ears
   C. Brain, eyes, legs   D. Brain, heart, eyes

6. Which organ removes waste and water from the blood?

A.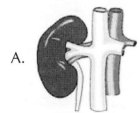

B.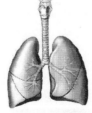

C.

D.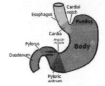

7. **Which of these foods give us energy?**

A.

B.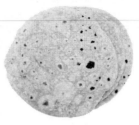

C.

D. B and C both

8. **We need _____ to protect our body.**

A.

B.

C.

D. All the above

9. **Which of these organs give us the sense of touch?**

A. Tongue   B. Skin

C. Ear   D. Eye

10. Identify the human organ system given below:

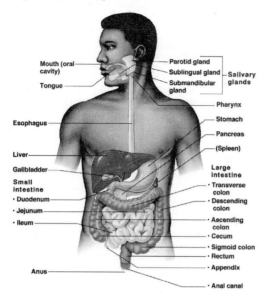

A. Circulatory system   B. Respiratory system
C. Excretory system   D. Digestive system

11. **Which of the following structures of a house can be flat, slopping, or semi-circular?**
    A. Roof   B. Floor
    C. Door   D. Mud

12. **Eskimos live in:**
    A. Huts   B. Caravans
    C. House boats   D. Igloos

13. **Observe the given image and identify the organism from which the following fibre is obtained:**
    A. Worm
    B. Rabbit
    C. Snake
    D. Goat

14. **Clothes are made from:**
    A. Web   B. Fibre
    C. Barks   D. Microbes

15. **Eid is celebrated every year as _____.**
    A. Eid-ul-Zulha   B. Eid-ul-Fitr
    C. Eid-ul-Milad   D. All of them

16. Look at the following picture carefully. Which occasion in the Hindu family is shown in the picture?

    A. Housewarming   B. Wedding

    C. Anniversary   D. Birthday

17. Ananya is Gaurav's sister. Gaurav is Shruti's father. What will Shruti call Ananya?

    A. Aunt   B. Sister

    C. Mother   D. Sister-in-law

18. Potentially, a person is half similar to his/her _____.

    A. Sibling   B. Father

    C. Mother   D. All of them

19. This person brings letters and parcels:

    A. Nurse   B. Postman

    C. Doctor   D. Police

20. A musician does not use which of these items?

A.    B.

C.    D.

21. **Which of the following is a wrong statement?**
    A. Walk on the footpath
    B. We must stand in a queue at the bus stop
    C. Do not get in or out of the moving bus
    D. Do not obey the traffic rules

22. **How many means of transport are hidden in the given word grid?**

```
S T R U C K
B U S C A R
O T R A I N
I S H I P O
U B O A T F
```

    A. 4   B. 5
    C. 6   D. 7

23. **In the following figure, what is Q?**

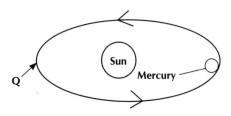

    A. Revolution   B. Track
    C. Orbit   D. Axis

24. **A piece of land surrounded by water on three sides is called _____.**
    A. Continent   B. Peninsula
    C. Island   D. Plateau

25. **Which of these colours is not found in the rainbow?**
    A. Yellow   B. Black
    C. Red   D. Blue

Answer Key

1. A   2. A   3. C   4. B   5. C   6. A   7. D   8. D   9. B 10.
D 11. A   12. D   13. A   14. B   15. D   16. B   17. A   18. A   19. B 20.
B 21. D 22. C   23. C   24. B   25. B

Achievers Section

1. **Match the columns and select the correct options.**

I	II
a. Stomach	1. Pumps blood to all parts of the body
b. Brain	2. Helps us breathe
c. Lungs	3. Helps us in digestion
d. Heart	4. Helps us think and remember

   A. a-2; b-4; c-1; d-3
   B. a-2; b-1; c-4; d-3
   C. a-4; b-2; c-1; d-3
   D. a-2, b-4, c-3, d-1

2. **Match column I with column II and select the correct options.**

Column I (Animal)	Column-II (Home)
a. Bee	1. Web
b. Rabbit	2. Stable
c. Spider	3. Kennel
d. Horse	4. Hive
e. Dog	5. Burrow

   A. a-1; b-2; c-3; d-4; e-5
   B. a-4; b-5; c-1; d-2; e-3
   C. a-1; b-5; c-3; d-4; e-2
   D. a-2; b-5; c-1; d-4; e-3

3. **What is X and Y in the given rhyme about traffic signals?**

   > Twinkle, twinkle traffic light
   > Shining on the corner bright.
   > When it's 'X' it's time to go;
   > When it's 'Z' it's time to STOP! you know.
   > Twinkle, twinkle traffic light
   > Shining on the corner bright.
   > "Stop!' says the 'Z' light,
   > "Go!' says the 'Y'.
   > "Wait!' says the 'P',
   > Till the light is 'X'.

	X	Y
A.	Red	Yellow
B.	Yellow	Red
C.	Green	Green

4. Guess what happened?

These sentences tell a story, but they are in the wrong order. Write them in the correct order.

1. He fell into it.
2. He did not see the hole.
3. A bus stopped and an old man got off.
4. Yesterday some men dug a hole.

A. 1, 2, 3, and 4   B. 4, 1, 2, and 3
C. 3, 2, 4, and 1   D. 4, 3, 2, and 1

5. Look at the picture below carefully.

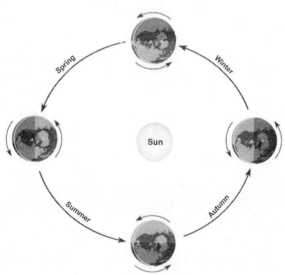

Now answer the following questions.

I. What causes the Sun to rise and set every day?

II. Which of these is most responsible for the changes of the seasons on Earth?

	I	II
A.	Orbit of the Earth	Position of the Moon
B.	Rotation of the Earth	Tilt of Earth on its axis
C.	Revolution of the Earth	Temperature of the Sun
D.	Rotation of the Earth	Rotation of the Earth

Answer Key

1. **A**; 2. **B**; 3. **C**; 4. **D**; 5. **B**

Maths Olympiad

Numbers ★ Addition ★ Subtraction ★ Measurement ★ Time ★ Money ★ Geometrical Shapes ★ Patterns ★ Odd One Out ★ Series Completion ★ Analogy ★ Ranking Test ★ Problems Based on Figures ★ High Order Thinking Skills ★ Model Paper – 1 ★ Model Paper – 2

Numbers Sense ★ Addition and Subtraction ★ Multiplication ★ Division ★ Measurement ★ Time, Calendar, and Temperature ★ Money ★ Geometrical Shapes ★ Pattern ★ Series Completion ★ Classification ★ Problems Based on Figures ★ High Order Thinking Skills ★ Model Test Paper – 1 ★ Model Test Paper – 2

★ Number System ★ Addition ★ Subtraction ★ Multiplication ★ Division ★ Fractions ★ Weight ★ Capacity ★ Time ★ Money ★ Geometrical Shapes ★ Pattern ★ Series Completion ★ Odd One Out ★ Coding and Decoding ★ Alphabet Test and Word Formation ★ Problems Based on Figures ★ High Order Thinking Skills ★ Model Test Paper – 1 ★ Model Test Paper – 2

★ Number System ★ Roman Numerals ★ Addition ★ Subtraction ★ Multiplication ★ Division ★ Factors and Multiples ★ Fractions ★ Measurement ★ Money ★ Time and Calendar ★ Geometry ★ Series and Pattern ★ Coding and Decoding ★ Number Ranking and Alphabet Test ★ Direction Sense Test ★ Mirror and Water Images ★ Pictorial Representation of Data ★ Mathematical and Analytical Reasoning ★ High Order Thinking Skills ★ Model Test Paper – 1 ★ Model Test Paper – 2 ★ Model Test Paper – 3

★ Number System ★ Roman Numbers ★ Operations on Numbers ★ Decimals and Fractions ★ LCM and HCF ★ Ratio and Proportion ★ Measurement ★ Temperature ★ Money ★ Area, Perimeter and Volume ★ Geometrical Shapes and Angles ★ Series and Pattern ★ Analogy ★ Odd One Out ★ Coding and Decoding ★ Number Ranking and Alphabet Test ★ Direction Sense Test ★ Mirror and Water Images ★ Pictorial Representation of Data ★ High Order Thinking Skills ★ Model Test Paper – 1 ★ Model Test Paper – 2

Maths Olympiad

Playing with Numbers ★ Number System ★ Integers ★ Fractions ★ Decimals ★ Simplification ★ Problems on Ages ★ Ratio and Proportion ★ Algebra ★ Mensuration ★ Geometry ★ Pattern ★ Analogy ★ Series Completion ★ Odd One Out ★ Coding Decoding ★ Alphabet Test ★ Number and Ranking Test ★ Direction Sense Test ★ Essential Element ★ Mirror Image ★ Embedded Figure ★ Figure Puzzles ★ High Order Thinking Skills (HOTS) ★ Short Answer Questions ★ Model Test Paper – 1

Number System ★ Rational Numbers ★ Integers ★ Decimals ★ Percentage ★ Surds and Indices ★ Simple Interest ★ Compound Interest ★ Profit and Loss ★ Algebraic Expressions ★ Linear Equations in One Variable ★ Lines and Angles ★ Triangle ★ Data Handling ★ Elementary Mensuration – I ★ Elementary Mensuration – II ★ Mathematical Reasoning ★ Pattern ★ Number Series ★ Alphabetical Series ★ Odd One Out ★ Coding Decoding ★ Alphabet Test ★ Blood Relation Test....

Playing with Numbers ★ Rational Numbers ★ Square and Square Roots ★ Cube and Cube Roots ★ Exponents and Powers ★ Profit and Loss ★ Algebraic Expressions and Their ★ Linear Equations in One Variable ★ Quadrilaterals ★ Mensuration ★ Visualising Solid Shapes ★ Data Handling ★ Direct and Inverse Variations ★ Alphabet Test ★ Odd One Out ★ Coding Decoding ★ Direction Sense Test ★ Series Completion ★ Pattern ★ Number Ranking ★ Analytical Reasoning ★ Venn Diagram ★ Embedded Figure ★ Completion of Incomplete Pattern ★ Water Images...

Number System ★ Polynomials ★ Co-ordinate Geometry ★ Linear Educations in Two Variables ★ Introduction to Euclid's Geometry ★ Lines and Angles ★ Triangles ★ Quadrilaterals ★ Area of Parallelograms and Triangles ★ Circles ★ Heron's Formula ★ Surface Area and Volume ★ Statistics ★ Probability ★ Analogy ★ Classification ★ Series Completion ★ Coding and Decoding ★ Number, Ranking, and Time Sequence Test ★ Alphabet Test ★ Blood Relation Test ★ Mathematical Operations ★ Arithmetical Reasoning....

Real Numbers ★ Polynomials ★ Linear Equations in Two Variables ★ Quadratic Equations ★ Arithmetic Progression ★ Triangles ★ Co-ordinate Geometry ★ Trigonometry ★ Circles ★ Surface Area and Volume ★ Statistics ★ Probability ★ Analogy ★ Classification ★ Coding and Decoding ★ Number, Ranking, and Time ★ Sequence Test ★ Direction Sense Test ★ Alphabet Test ★ Blood Relation Test ★ Mathematical Operations ★ Series ★ Paper Folding ★ Paper Cutting ★ Mirror Images ★ High Order Thinking Skills (HOTS)....

Science Olympiad

Science Olympiad

Measurement of Distances and Motion ★ Light, Shadows and Reflections ★ Electricity and Circuits ★ Fun with Magnets ★ Air and Water ★ Sorting and Separation of Materials ★ Changes Around Us ★ Living Organisms and Their Surroundings ★ Food, Health and Hygiene ★ Fibre to Fabric ★ Pattern ★ Analogy ★ Series Completion ★ Odd One Out ★ Coding – Decoding ★ Alphabet Test ★ Number and Ranking Test ★ Direction Sense Test...

Heat and Temperature ★ Motion and Time ★ Electric Current and Its Effects ★ Winds, Storms and Cyclones ★ Light Acids, Bases and Salts ★ Physical and Chemical Changes ★ Weather, Climate and Adaptations of Animals ★ Fibres to Fabrics ★ Nutrition in Plants and Animals ★ Respiration in Organisms ★ Transport and Excretion ★ Reproduction in Plants ★ Natural Resources and Their Conservation ★ Pattern ★ Number Series...

Force and Pressure ★ Friction ★ Light ★ Sound ★ Chemical Effects of Electric Current ★ Stars and the Solar System ★ Some Natural Phenomena ★ Metals and Non-Metals ★ Combustion and Flame ★ Coal and Petroleum ★ Synthetic Fibres and Plastics ★ Cell-Structure and Functions ★ Microorganisms ★ Reproduction in Animals ★ Crop Production and Management ★ Conservation of Plants and Animals ★ Pollution of Air and Water ★ Alphabet Test ★ Odd and Out ★ Coding-Decoding ★ Direction Sense Test ★ Series Completion ★ Pattern ★ Number Ranking...

Motion ★ Force and Laws of Motion ★ Gravitation ★ Work and Energy ★ Sound ★ Matter in Our Surroundings ★ Is Matter Around us Pure ★ Atoms and Molecules ★ Structure of Atom ★ Cell-The Fundamental Unit of Life ★ Tissues ★ Diversity in Living Organisms ★ Why do We Fall Ill ★ Natural Resources ★ Improvement in Food Resources ★ Analogy ★ Classification ★ Series Completion ★ Coding and Decoding ★ Number, Ranking, and Time Sequence Test ★ Alphabet Test ★ Blood Relation ★ Mathematical Operations.

Light ★ Human Eye and Colourful World ★ Electricity ★ Magnetic Effects of Electric Current ★ Sources of Energy ★ Chemical Reactions and Equations ★ Acids, Bases and Salts ★ Metals and Non-Metals ★ Carbon and Its Compounds ★ Periodic Classification of Elements ★ Life Processes ★ Reproduction in Organism ★ Heredity and Evolution ★ Our Environment ★ Analogy ★ Classification ★ Coding and Decoding ★ Number, Ranking, and Time Sequence Test ★ Direction Sense Test ★ Alphabet Test ★ Blood Relation....

visit our online bookstore: **www.vspublishers.com**

Cyber Olympiad

* Introduction to Computer
* Fundamentals of Computer
* Parts of Computer
* Uses of Computer
* Learning to Use Keyboard
* Learning to Use Mouse
* Introduction to MS Paint ∗ Latest Developments in IT ∗ Patterns
* Odd One Out
* Series Completion
* Analogy
* Coding and Decoding
* Ranking Test
* Embedded Figures
* Grouping of Figures
* Measuring Units
* Geometrical Shapes
* High Order Thinking Skills
* Short Answer Questions
* Model Test Paper

* Fundamentals of Computer
* Generations of Computer
* MS Paint
* MS Word 2010
* Introduction to Internet
* Latest Development in IT
* Patterns
* Odd One Out
* Series Completion
* Analogy and Classification
* Coding and Decoding
* Ranking and Alphabet Test
* Mirror and Water Images
* Days, Dates and Time
* Geometrical Shapes
* High Order Thinking Skills
* Short Answer Questions
* Model Test Paper

* Fundamentals of Computer
* Evolution of Computer
* MS Word 2010
* MS Paint ∗ Network
* Internet and Its Uses ∗ Windows 7
* Latest Developments in IT ∗ Patterns
* Analogy and Classification
* Coding and Decoding
* Alphabet and Ranking Test
* Direction Sense Test ∗ Mirror and Water Images
* Geometrical Shapes and Solids
* Time and Calendar
* High Order Thinking Skills
* Short Answer Questions
* Model Test Paper

* Fundamentals of Computer
* Memory and Storage Devices
* Introduction to Multimedia
* MS Paint ∗ MS Word 2010 ∗ MS PowerPoint 2010
* Windows 7
* Network
* Internet
* Latest Development in IT
* Patterns ∗ Analogy and Classification
* Coding and Decoding
* Ranking and Alphabet Test
* Direction Sense Test ∗ Mirror and Water Images
* Geometrical Shapes and Angles ∗ High Order Thinking Skills ∗ Short Answer Questions
* Model Test Paper

Cyber Olympiad

Evolution of Computer ★ Fundamentals of Computer ★ MS Windows 7 ★ MS Word 2010 ★ MS PowerPoint 2010 ★ Introduction to Qbasic ★ Internet and E-mail ★ Latest Developments in Field of IT ★ Analogy ★ Odd One Out ★ Alphabet Test ★ Blood Relation Test ★ Direction Sense Test ★ Seating Arrangement ★ Syllogism and Venn Diagram ★ Mirror Images and Water Images ★ Embedded Figures ★ Figure Matrix ★ High Order Thinking Skills ★ Short Answer Questions ★ Model Test Paper 1 & 2

Fundamentals of Computer ★ Evolution of Computer ★ MS Word 2010 ★ MS Excel 2010 ★ MS PowerPoint 2010 ★ Programming in Qbasic ★ Internet and Viruses ★ Latest Development in IT ★ Analogy ★ Odd One Out ★ Alphabet Test ★ Blood Relation Test ★ Direction Sense Test ★ Seating Arrangement ★ Syllogism ★ Embedded Figures ★ Figures Puzzles ★ Venn Diagram ★ Analytical Reasoning ★ High Order Thinking Skills ★ Short Answer Questions ★ Model Test Paper 1 & 2

Hardware and Software ★ Input, Output and Storage Devices ★ Networking ★ MS Word ★ MS PowerPoint ★ MS Excel ★ MS Access ★ HTML ★ Flash Cs6 ★ Internet and Viruses ★ Latest Developments in IT ★ Odd One Out ★ Series Completion ★ Coding and Decoding ★ Mathematical Reasoning ★ Amalytical Reasoning ★ Mirror Images ★ Embedded Figures ★ Problems Based on Figures ★ High Order Thinking Skills ★ Short Answer Questions ★ Model Test Paper 1 & 2

Algorithms and Flowchats ★ Visual Basic ★ Flash and Animations ★ HTML ★ Hardware and Software ★ Input and Output Devices ★ Memory and Storage Devices ★ MS Word ★ MS Excel ★ MS PowerPoint ★ Networking ★ Internet and Viruses ★ Latest Developments in IT ★ Analogy ★ Series Completion ★ Odd One Out ★ Coding and Decoding ★ Direction Sense Test ★ Number, Ranking and Time Sequence Test ★ Alphabet Test ★ Blood Relation Test ★ Problems Based on Figures ★ Analytical Reasoning...

★ Fundamentals of Computer ★ Input and Output Devices ★ Word Processing Tool ★ MS PowerPoint ★ MS Excal ★ HTML ★ MS Access ★ Networking and Multimedia ★ Internet ★ Basics of Information Technology ★ Analogy ★ Classification ★ Series Completion ★ C o d i n g Decoding ★ Alphabet Test and Number Ranking ★ Blood Relation Test ★ Direction Sense Test ★ Calendar ★ Series ★ Figure Pattern ★ Cubes and Dice ★ Mirror Images and Water Images ★ High Order Thinking Skills...

RAPIDEX ENGLISH SPEAKING COURSE/EXCEL ENGLISH SPEAKING COURSE

SBN : 9789381448908
(Telugu)

ISBN : 9789381448915
(Bangla)

ISBN : 9789381448922
(Oriya)

ISBN : 9789381448939
(Assamese)

ISBN : 9789381448946
(Nepalese)

Published in sixteen languages
Hindi, Malayalam, Tamil, Telugu, Kannada, Marathi, Gujarati, Bangla, Oriya, Urdu, Assamese, Punjabi, Nepalese, Persian, Arabic and Sinhalese

REGIONAL LANGUAGE/SPOKEN ENGLISH/LEARNING COURSES

: 9789357940054 (Bangla) | ISBN : 9789357940016 (Bangla) | ISBN :9789357940023 (Bangla) | ISBN : 9789357940085 (Bangla) | ISBN : 9789357940825 (Bangla) | ISBN : 9789357940092 (Bangla) | ISBN : 9789357940009 (Bangla) | ISBN : 9789357940030 (Bangla) | ISBN : 9789357941303 *(2 Colour Book)*

N : 9789357940061 (Bangla) | ISBN : 9789357940047 (Bangla) | ISBN : 9788122310924 (Bangla) | ISBN : 9789357940078 (Bangla) | ISBN 9789350570357 (Kannada) | ISBN : 9789350571200 (Kannada) | ISBN : 9789350570340 (Kannada) | ISBN : 9789350570944 (Kannada) | *(Coming Soon)*

N : 9789350570951 (Kannada) | ISBN : 9789350571309 (Kannada) | ISBN : 9789350571828 (Gujarati) | ISBN : 9789350571781 (Gujarati) | ISBN : 9789350571811 (Marathi) | ISBN : 9789350571804 (Marathi) | ISBN : 9789381384138 (Tamil) | ISBN : 9789381384121 (Tamil) | *(Coming Soon)*

: 9789357940153 Eng.-Bangla) | ISBN : 9789357940399 (Eng.-Kannada) | ISBN : 9789357940375 (Eng.-Odia) | ISBN : 9789357940382 (Eng.-Telugu) | ISBN : 9789357941358 (Eng.-Malayalam) | ISBN : 9789357941327 (Eng.-Tamil) | ISBN : 9789357940856 (Eng.-Marathi) | ISBN : 9789357940849 (Eng.-Gujarati) | ISBN : 9789357941334 (Eng.-Assamese)

9789357941341 Eng.-Urdu) | ISBN : 9789350570760 (Telugu) | ISBN : 9789350570098 (Telugu) | ISBN : 9789350571699 (Bangla) | ISBN : 9789350571125 (Bangla) | ISBN : 9789357940146 (Kannada) | ISBN : 9789357940139 (Kannada) | ISBN : 9789350571620 (Odia) | ISBN : 9789350571118 (Odia)

V&S OLYMPIAD SERIES FOR CLASSES 1-10

MATHS OLYMPIAD (CLASS 1-10)

ISBN : 9789357940504   ISBN : 9789357940511   ISBN : 9789357940528   ISBN : 9789357940535   ISBN : 9789357940542

ISBN : 9789357940559   ISBN : 9789357940566   ISBN : 9789357940573   ISBN : 9789357940580   ISBN : 9789357940597

SCIENCE OLYMPIAD (CLASS 1-10)

ISBN : 9789357940405   ISBN : 9789357940412   ISBN : 9789357940429   ISBN : 9789357940436   ISBN : 9789357940443

ISBN : 9789357940450   ISBN : 9789357940467   ISBN : 9789357940474   ISBN : 9789357940481   ISBN : 9789357940498

CYBER OLYMPIAD (CLASS 1-10)

ISBN : 9789357942102   ISBN : 9789357940603   ISBN : 9789357940610   ISBN : 9789357940627   ISBN : 9789357940634

ISBN : 9789357940641   ISBN : 9789357940658   ISBN : 9789357940665   ISBN : 9789357940672   ISBN : 9789357940689

ENGLISH OLYMPIAD (CLASS 1-10)

ISBN : 9789357940696   ISBN : 9789357940702   ISBN : 9789357940719   ISBN : 9789357940726   ISBN : 9789357940733

ISBN : 9789357940740   ISBN : 9789357940757   ISBN : 9789357940764   ISBN : 9789357940771   ISBN : 9789357940788

OLYMPIAD ONLINE TEST PACKAGE (CLASS 1-10)

ISBN : 9789357941754   ISBN : 9789357941761   ISBN : 9789357941778   ISBN : 978935794

ISBN : 9789357941792   ISBN : 9789357941808   ISBN : 9789357941815   ISBN : 978935794

ISBN : 9789357941839   ISBN : 9789357941846

**OLYMPIAD ONLINE TEST PACKAGE
CLASS 1-10
with CD with Activation Voucher
web Portal: www.vsexamprep.co**

OLYMPIAD COMBO PACK (4 BOOK SET)

ISBN : 9789357942003   ISBN : 9789357942010   ISBN : 978935794201

ISBN : 9789357942034   ISBN : 9789357942041   ISBN : 978935794201

ISBN : 9789357942065   ISBN : 9789357942072   ISBN : 978935794201

**CLASS 1-10 ENGLISH, MATH
CYBER, SCIENCE OLYMPIA
4 BOOKS SAVER COMBO PA**

ISBN : 9789357942096

CAREER & BUSINESS/SELF-HELP/PERSONALITY DEVELOPMENT/STRESS MANAGEMENT

 ISBN : 9789381588789
 ISBN : 9789350571637
 ISBN : 9789381588512
 ISBN : 9789381588963
 ISBN : 9789381588598
 ISBN : 9789381384039
 ISBN : 9788192079622
 ISBN : 9789350570753
 ISBN : 9789381384396

 ISBN : 9789381384541
 ISBN : 9789350570968
 ISBN : 9789381384527
ISBN : 9789381588666
ISBN : 9789381384541
ISBN : 9789381384107
ISBN : 9789350571187
ISBN : 9789381588574
ISBN : 9789381588277

 ISBN : 9789381588222
 ISBN : 9789381384213
 ISBN : 9789381588772
 ISBN : 9789381588949
  ISBN : 9789357940108
 ISBN : 9789381384152
 ISBN : 9789381384145
 ISBN : 9789381448564
 ISBN : 9789381384473

 ISBN : 9789381448595
 ISBN : 9789381448670
 ISBN : 9789381588253
 ISBN : 9789381448755
 ISBN : 9789381448649
 ISBN : 9789381384480
 ISBN : 9789350571309
 ISBN : 9789381448632
 ISBN : 9789381384893

 ISBN : 9789381384091
ISBN : 9789381384176
ISBN : 9789350570265
ISBN : 9789381588727
ISBN : 9789350570128
ISBN : 9789381588246
ISBN : 9789381448687
ISBN : 9789381448786
ISBN : 9789381448533

 ISBN : 9789381448526
 ISBN : 9789381384206
 ISBN : 9788122310689
 ISBN : 9789381384503
 ISBN : 9789381588505
 ISBN : 9789381448717
 ISBN : 9788192079646
 ISBN : 9789350570203
 ISBN : 9789350570272

 ISBN : 9789381588741
 ISBN : 9789350571170
 ISBN : 9789381588215
 ISBN : 9789381384763
 ISBN : 9789350570296
 ISBN : 9789381588284
 ISBN : 9789381588543
 ISBN : 9789350571880
 ISBN : 9789381588765

 ISBN : 9789350570579
 ISBN : 9789350571927
 ISBN : 9789350571545
ISBN : 9789381384114
ISBN : 9789381384435
ISBN : 9789381448779
ISBN : 9789381448991
ISBN : 9789381384510
ISBN : 9789381384169
ISBN : 9789350570623

All Books Available on Flipkart, Amazon, Infibeam, Snapdeal, Shopcluse • marketing@vspublishers.com

ISBN : 9789357941310   ISBN : 9789357941495   ISBN : 9789381384053   ISBN : 9789381384060   ISBN : 9789381384121   ISBN : 9788122310924   ISBN : 9789381588468   ISBN : 9789381588604   ISBN : 978935057

ISBN : 9789350570470   ISBN : 9789350570487   ISBN : 9789350570500   ISBN : 9789350570586   ISBN : 9789350571248   ISBN : 9789350571248   ISBN : 9789350571743   ISBN : 9789381384299   ISBN : 978938144

ISBN : 9789381384305   ISBN : 9789381384954   ISBN : 9789381588819   ISBN : 9789350570371   ISBN : 9789350570388   ISBN : 9789350570395   ISBN : 9789350570401   ISBN : 9789350570364   ISBN : 978938158

ISBN : 9789381448977   ISBN : 9789381384459   ISBN : 9789381384930   ISBN : 9789350571682   ISBN : 9789381588864   ISBN : 9789381588673   ISBN : 9789350570111   ISBN : 9789381384312   ISBN : 978938158

ISBN : 9789350570258   ISBN : 9789350570227   ISBN : 9789381588499   ISBN : 9789381588338   ISBN : 9789381588345   ISBN : 9789381448656   ISBN : 9789381384558   ISBN : 9788192079639   ISBN : 9789350

ISBN : 9789350571026   ISBN : 9789350571033   ISBN : 9789350571040   ISBN : 9789350571057   ISBN : 9789350570999   ISBN : 9789350571002   ISBN : 9789350571064   ISBN : 9789350571071   ISBN : 978935057

ISBN : 9789350571101   ISBN : 9789381588321   ISBN : 9789381588307   ISBN : 9789381588567   ISBN : 9789350571163   ISBN : 9789350570517   ISBN : 9789381384183   ISBN : 9789381448625   ISBN : 978938

ISBN : 9789381384190   ISBN : 9789381448793   ISBN : 9789381588192   ISBN : 9789381588802   ISBN : 9789381588970   ISBN : 9789350570777   ISBN : 9789381448427   ISBN : 9789350570555   ISBN : 97893

FUN. FACT & MAGIC/TALES & STORIES/LEISURE READING

ISBN : 9788192079660   ISBN : 9788192079677   ISBN : 9789381588659   ISBN : 9789381588840   ISBN : 9789381588857   ISBN : 9789381588871   ISBN : 9789381588888   ISBN : 9789381384336   ISBN : 9789381448069

ISBN : 9789381448090   ISBN : 9789381448083   ISBN : 9789381384343   ISBN : 9789381448076   ISBN : 9789381448809   ISBN : 9789381448885   ISBN : 9789350571248   ISBN : 9789350570210   ISBN : 9789381384329

ISBN : 9789381448229   ISBN : 9789381448236   ISBN : 9789350570227   ISBN : 9789381588697   ISBN : 9788192079608   ISBN : 9789350571644   ISBN : 9789381588734   ISBN : 9789350570180   ISBN : 9789381448168

ISBN : 9789381588314   ISBN : 9789381588260   ISBN : 9788192079691   ISBN : 9789381588291   ISBN : 9789381588956   ISBN : 9789350570852   ISBN : 9789350570906   ISBN : 9789350570838   ISBN : 9789350570883

ISBN : 9789350570845   ISBN : 9789350570890   ISBN : 9789350570869   ISBN : 9789350570913   ISBN : 9789350570821   ISBN : 9783950570876   ISBN : 9789350570920   ISBN : 9789350570937

ISBN : 9789381588987   ISBN : 9789350570005   ISBN : 9789350570012   ISBN : 9789350570029   ISBN : 9789381588994   ISBN : 9789350570036   ISBN : 9789350570043   ISBN : 9789350570050   ISBN : 9789381588406

ISBN : 9789381448182   ISBN : 9789381448199   ISBN : 9789381448144   ISBN : 9789381384404   ISBN : 9789381588451   ISBN : 9789381588581   ISBN : 9789381588529   ISBN : 9789381448137   ISBN : 9789381448106

ISBN : 9789381448175   ISBN : 9789381448113   ISBN : 9789381448120   ISBN : 9789381448151   ISBN : 9789381384701   ISBN : 9789381384718   ISBN : 9789381384862   ISBN : 9788192079615   ISBN : 9789381384015

HEALTH & BEAUTY CARE/FAMILY & RELATIONS/LIFESTYLE

ISBN : 9789350570463

ISBN : 9789381588482

ISBN : 9789381448724

ISBN : 9789381448762

ISBN : 9789381448823

ISBN : 9789381384961

ISBN : 9789381384442

ISBN : 9789381448496

ISBN : 97893815889

ISBN : 9788122307511

ISBN : 9789381448502

ISBN : 9789381384633

ISBN : 9789381448489

ISBN : 9789381384251

ISBN : 9789350570593

ISBN : 9789381384831

ISBN : 9789381384800

ISBN : 97893505706

ISBN : 9789381384220

ISBN : 9789381384817

ISBN : 9789381384572

ISBN : 9789381448694

ISBN : 9789381384824

ISBN : 9789381448565

ISBN : 9789381384909

ISBN : 9789350570609

ISBN : 978938144

ISBN : 9789381448458

ISBN : 9789381384589

ISBN : 9788192079653

ISBN : 9789381384978

ISBN : 9789381448472

ISBN : 9789381448731

ISBN : 9789350571897

ISBN : 9789381448434

ISBN : 978938144

ISBN : 9789381448244

ISBN : 9789381384237

ISBN : 9789381384626

ISBN : 9789381448519

ISBN : 9789381384619

ISBN : 9789381448892

ISBN : 9789381384602

ISBN : 9789381588369

ISBN : 978938158

ISBN : 9789381588383

ISBN : 9789381588390

ISBN : 9789381448557

ISBN : 9789381588826

ISBN : 9789381384268

ISBN : 9788122305159

ISBN : 9789381448748

ISBN : 9789381384992

ISBN : 978938138

ISBN : 9789381448700

ISBN : 9789381588758

ISBN : 9789381384923

ISBN : 9789350570104

ISBN : 9789381448618

ISBN : 9789381448441

ISBN : 9789381384688

ISBN : 9789381384282

ISBN : 9788122308

ISBN : 9789381384854

ISBN : 9789381384046

ISBN : 9789381384275

ISBN : 9789381384985

ISBN : 9789381448601

ISBN : 9789381448861

ISBN : 9789381384640

ISBN : 9789381384848

ISBN : 9789381384

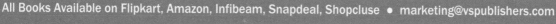